Magnetic
Reactive Magic Book Two
Helen Vivienne Fletcher

First published in this format by HVF Publishing in 2022
Copyright © Helen Vivienne Fletcher, 2022
Edited by Jess Senior

This is a work of fiction. Names, characters, businesses, places, events, locales, and incidents are either the products of the author's imagination or used in a fictitious manner. Any resemblance to actual persons, living or dead, or actual events is purely coincidental.

ISBN:
978-1-99-116720-0 (paperback)
978-1-99-116721-7 (mobi)
978-1-99-116722-4 (epub)
978-1-99-116723-1 (large print)

This one is for Ivana.

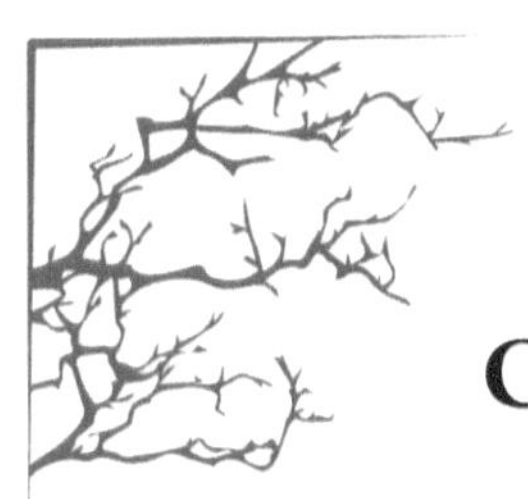

Chapter One

Callie

"**B**e a sunflower."

Toby's words filled me with a warm peaceful feeling.

"Be a sunflower," I repeated, hearing all of my classmates echo it too.

Toby's plant – the one that had been terrorising us for the last hour – disappeared. Instead, he stood in the centre of the room, magic flowing from him so intensely even I could see it. Around us, the chaos stopped, the wind calming and Zo's sparks burning out.

"You did it," I whispered.

He stared down at Miss Trager and Mr Grandace. They had survived being pulled into the centre of the siren plant, and I couldn't say I was entirely happy about it. They should have faced consequences for causing all this.

Zo laughed, and new sparks danced around her, shimmering like drops of water in a spider's web. Asher held Julianna as she cried tears of relief into his shoulder, and Elijah lay on the floor, simply breathing being all he could manage right now.

And then there was Toby, standing in the centre of all of it. He glowed, magic flowing through him. I looked down at my hands.

The same magic ran through me – through all of us, tying our bodies and minds together.

Words whispered inside my head, too fast to catch. I stepped back, confused by the swirling mix of voices – my classmates' thoughts – echoing through my mind.

Toby turned to me, his face euphoric. "I save you, you save me, right?" he said.

"Yeah..." I couldn't keep the hesitancy from my voice.

The threads of magic he'd sent to join us pulled tight around me. I pulled back, but they drew me in again, growing taught. Elijah strained against them too, wearing at the magic.

Suddenly I was laughing. The sound bubbled up inside me, but it didn't come from me. Zo and Julianna laughed too, the fluttering sound spreading.

Toby moved toward me, pulling me into a hug and then cupping my face in his hands. I stared at him, everything swirling. Out of the corner of my eye, I saw Miss Trager stand. She held a sunflower, and the petals wilted, the plant decaying faster than seemed possible.

Toby's fingers brushed my face, drawing my attention back to him. But the moment fractured. I saw it through six pairs of eyes. My own and Toby's, and all four of my other classmates watching. I lost myself, dizziness taking over. Magic crept over our skin, winding and twisting around us, like the crawling vines of his siren plant. They tightened, making it hard to breathe. Elijah pulled against them, resisting like I was.

And then, a snap.

Toby drew back, his eyes widening, and I felt mine mirror his. The laughter died in my lungs. I reached for the threads of magic and found only frayed ends.

"Toby?" His name cracked on my lips, my mouth suddenly dry.

He went pale, his eyes widening. "We have to go back," he whispered.

I GASPED, OPENING MY eyes. For a moment, I had no idea where I was; my dream of the school overtaking everything else. Then I heard Zo snoring softly in the bed across from me, and my eyes finally adjusted to the gloom.

Light crept in at the window, giving the frilly pink curtains a halo. Darkness obscured the walls, but I pictured the pale purple flowered wallpaper, a remnant from Zo's childhood, and the eclectic mix of pictures she'd covered it with. The strangeness of waking up here – of living in someone else's bedroom – settled over me, but I was safe... far away from the school.

Zo let out a shimmer of little sparks – red and gold ones, so she must have been dreaming something nice. They fluttered through the air, burning out before they landed – thank goodness. She'd gotten better at controlling her emotional magical manifestations – magistations as she and Toby called them – but sometimes they still became unruly. Both our beds held scorch marks from when she'd had nightmares a few weeks ago.

I covered my face with my hands, willing my breath and heart rate to slow. If I kept quiet and calm, perhaps I could avoid dragging the others awake.

I'm safe, I said to myself. *It's okay.*

Zo stirred in her sleep, and I looked over at her. A selfish part of me wanted her to wake up. Her reassurance would probably take the form of an unimpressed shrug and sarcastic comment, but still... Funny how things had changed. It seemed strange now that I'd once seen Zo, and my other classmates, as the enemy.

I reached out, feeling for the magic. The thread connecting me to Toby held strong, winding across my skin like swirling tattoos, but only torn edges remained of the one which had tied me to Elijah. The sensation of it snapping burned raw in my mind.

Zo's breathing fell back into the regular pattern of sleep, and the heaviness of my former classmates' dreams washed over me. I lay still, hoping the calmness would rub off on me, but instead my heart tap danced on the inside of my chest. Though I was only tied to Toby, he was also tied to Zo, and she to Julianna, and so on. If I wasn't careful, I would wake them, despite the miles between us, my emotions travelling down the line until all six of us were wide-eyed, staring at the clock. Every action was like a strange, long-distance game of dominos.

I slipped out of bed, grabbing a hoodie and my phone. I bundled the limp, sweaty coils of my hair up into a bun, and padded softly across the wooden floorboards in the hallway, making my way down the stairs. Classmates aside, Zo's parents would not be impressed if I woke them up crashing around at 3am.

I opened the front door, stopping at the threshold. I itched to be outside, to take a cold breath of night air and stare up at the sky, but even so, I found myself tensing at the thought of taking that last step.

I'm safe, I said to myself. *Nothing is blocking me from leaving.*

Still, I couldn't help but look down, inspecting the doorstep for rune lines. I imagined shackles appearing as soon as I stepped over it, and I had to touch my wrists to reassure myself that the bracelets the school had made me wear were gone. I wasn't a prisoner anymore. We'd left the school three months ago, but it still followed me into my dreams almost every night, and the echoes of my time there filled my days. I swallowed, then stepped through the doorway into the night.

The tension in my body eased as soon as I did. I looked up, breathing in. Being able to see the stars always helped. I sat down on the lawn, ignoring the dew creeping through my pyjamas, and closed my eyes. I cupped my palms in front of me and pictured starting a small fire in my hands – just enough to warm me. Zo would have been able to do it. Even Toby probably could have given it a shot. His magic had gotten stronger since he tied the six of us together, though it remained unpredictable. Mine hadn't. I could feel and see the magic in ways I hadn't been able to before, but I still didn't have control of it. My hands stayed determinedly empty.

I opened my eyes and blinked. Something orange caught my eye, and my stomach lurched – setting fire to the garden was the last thing I needed. But it was a sunflower, peeking up from between Zo's mum's roses. Once upon a time, I'd found them beautiful; now the sight of them reminded me of Miss Trager and filled me with a nauseating mix of anxiety and rage.

My phone beeped in my pocket. A message from Toby.

- YOU OKAY?

Of course he had woken with me, despite my efforts to avoid rousing him. YEAH, JUST A NIGHTMARE.

There was a pause, then my phone lit up again.

- I KNOW. IT BUMS ME OUT YOU KEEP HAVING NIGHTMARES ABOUT ME HUGGING YOU.

He followed that up with "lol", but I cringed at the thought of him seeing that. Nothing was private, not even our dreams.

- THAT WASN'T THE SCARY PART! I wrote back.

I'm not sure why I kept dreaming about that last day at the school. Sure, it had been terrifying at the time, but we had survived it. Honestly, I couldn't even put my finger on exactly what about the dream unsettled me so much. I'd had much worse ones, and so had the others. Last night, Toby dreamt of the fireball Miss Trager had tried to kill him with, and we'd both woken to our skin burning with sweat. Still, something about the urgency in dream-Toby's voice... the sudden fear on his face... It all unnerved me in a way I couldn't quite explain.

It's okay, Callie. Toby's voice sounded in my head.

My breath caught, and I let it out slowly. I'd never get used to being able to read his mind.

You're safe, he thought. *We never have to go back.*

He moved his hand, gently folding his fingers down as if encompassing mine. I did the same, imagining we were next to each other, our fingers intertwined.

My phone lit up again.

- VISIT TOMORROW?

I smiled. He didn't need to message; I could hear his thoughts as naturally as my own. He did it because he knew it made me feel more normal – a pretence that I could actually control what I communicated and when.

My smile fell. CAN'T, I wrote back.

I could feel how much he missed me, the magical thread between us pulling tight every time he moved, despite him being over two hours' drive away. I missed him too, but tomorrow was Zo's little brother's birthday party and I'd promised I would help.

I didn't tell him it was my birthday too – my seventeenth. I hoped I'd buried that deep enough within myself that even the magic couldn't find it.

He sent back a sad face and I imagined squeezing his hand. I wished they were all there with me. It's not like I wanted to go back to the six of us sleeping in one room again, but after everything that happened, it was almost painful to be apart. Sometimes I could almost see the chain of magical ties stretching between me and my former classmates, even now with the miles between us. Then I would blink, and it would disappear, leaving me with just the taut, physical sensation of it pulling tight.

I sighed and opened my eyes, almost ready to go back inside. My breath caught. A man stood across the street staring at me. For a moment, I thought it was our former principal, and my muscles tensed, ready for an attack.

You okay? I heard Toby's voice, but it crackled like a bad phone connection.

The man wasn't Mr Grandace – his greying hair and superior height told me that – but he was still a stranger standing outside Zo's house, staring at me, in the middle of the night.

I forced a smile, raising my hand into a wave. The man didn't smile back, and unease crept over me. He took a step towards me. I scrambled up, backing towards the house.

Toby!

Static filled my head, blocking out his voice. My phone beeped, and I jumped, dropping it. I fumbled, but the phone fell to the ground. I left it there.

I looked up. The man was gone. I scanned the street, searching for him. Nothing. A dog barked further down, and I started again, spinning around to look for it.

A figure drifted towards the corner, a black Labrador pausing to sniff something beside him. I let out a breath, watching it crystalise in the air in front of me. Of course. He hadn't been staring at me, but at the dog hidden in the shadows. I started to laugh, and I felt Toby do the same.

Gave me a fright there, Reactive Girl. His voice came through clear, the static gone.

"I think I gave myself one," I said aloud.

I picked up my phone, checking it for damage, then opened the message – a group one from Elijah.

- ANY CHANCE YOU TWO WILL SHUT UP
  AND LET ME GET SOME SLEEP SOON?

Damn. Our conversation must be echoing all the way down the line if even Elijah had been woken by it.

- SORRY! I messaged the group.

My phone beeped with replies from Asher and Julianna, acknowledging my apology. They were too sleep-riddled to make much sense.

I glanced down the street again. The man had disappeared for real this time, taking the dog around the corner. Without meaning to, my hand had crept to my wrist, checking for the bracelets which had kept me prisoner.

Relax, I said to myself once more. *You're safe here.*

The front door behind me creaked, and Zo appeared in the entryway, rubbing her eyes.

"You okay?" she asked.

I nodded. "Sorry, I didn't mean to wake everyone."

She shrugged. "We've all done it before."

She reached out a hand to me. I hesitated, not quite ready to give up the peaceful feeling of being outside, though the dog walker had already ruined that. I wondered how long it would take for us all to start feeling normal again, or at least, normal apart from the magic.

I could feel Toby's eyes closing, slipping towards sleep. Beyond him, the others were on the verge of it too, only awake because my nightmare had set off the chain reaction.

Night, Toby, I said inside my head.

Dream well, Callie, he whispered back.

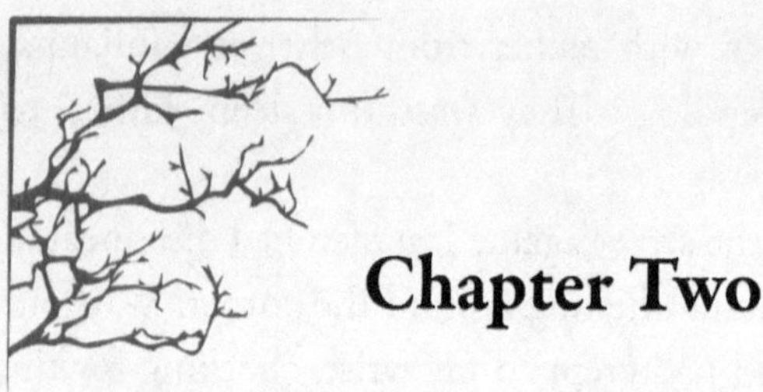

Chapter Two

Zo and I woke late the next morning. She hit the snooze button so many times it stopped ringing, and I'd turned my phone off after the first chime. Her mum eventually came in to wake us, and I dragged myself off to the shower. Zo lay on her back, getting only so far as to flop one foot out of bed.

I felt for her. Toby and the others were still asleep. Just as one of us waking suddenly could drag the others to consciousness, one being deeply asleep could pull us all back down again. The balance was not in our favour this morning. I only had the connection to Toby, and that made me feel like one of my limbs was still asleep. For Zo, being connected to Toby on one side and Julianna on the other, it would be like trying to wake from an anaesthetic.

I headed downstairs, giving up on trying to get Zo out of bed. Every so often, images from Toby's dreams flickered through my mind, and I'd have to pause, doing nothing but breathing until the real world came back into focus. I stepped off the last stair just as Josh ran down the hallway, looking back over his shoulder.

"Watch it, Josh!" I grabbed his shoulders, steadying both of us before he crashed into my hip. He backed away a pace, staring at me.

I forced my face into a smile. "Guess I should wish you a happy birthday?" It came out sounding sarcastic, which wasn't what I meant.

Josh went quiet, his eyes growing wide. He was like that around me. Fair enough – I wasn't his sister, just some strange girl Zo had brought home with her from school – but the stares made me nervous, and prickliness crept into my voice. Of course, that only made him shyer, and the cycle began again.

A frown appeared between his eyebrows, and he ran off. I sighed, closing my eyes. Hopefully the gift I'd got him would make it up to him.

I headed to the kitchen. Outside the window, a blackbird picked at the sunflower, pulling seeds from its centre. It was starting to wilt, turning brown and diseased looking, though the one next to it was still bright and cheerful. Strangely, I'd never noticed Zo's mum grew sunflowers. I guess the nightmare had me looking for them.

I poured bowls of cereal for me and Zo, then opened the fridge. The milk carton felt light. I weighed it in my hand, estimating how much was left. Had Zo's mum finished all the baking for the party? I decided not to risk it, eating my cereal dry instead.

Zo finally appeared, with one of her eyes scrunched up, letting in only the tiniest crack of light. "Morning…" she mumbled.

She picked up the bowl I'd left for her, then opened the fridge. My mouth was full of dry flakes, and she poured out the milk before I could stop her.

Zo's mum, Angela, popped her head around the kitchen door. "I've got to run to the store for a few things. Can I leave you two to froof up the cupcakes?" She flapped her hand at a plate of naked cupcakes on the bench.

I nodded, shoving another spoonful of dry cereal into my mouth.

"Sure, Mum." Zo stifled another yawn. "Can you get milk? I used the last of it."

"And left Callie without any?" Angela frowned.

Zo glanced over at my bowl, but I shook my head. "It's fine. I like it this way."

Zo scoffed. "No, you don't. Here." She flicked her hand, and a bubble of milk rose out of her bowl, landing with a splash in mine.

I blinked. Even after being surrounded by it at the school, magic still had the power to leave me speechless. "Thanks..." I wiped drops of milk from my shirt. "Maybe next time just pour it, though?"

Zo gave me a sleepy grin.

Angela had gone still, and the frown on her forehead deepened. "You know there can't be any magic in front of the guests, right?" She lowered her voice as if discussing something distasteful.

Zo rolled her eyes. "Of course."

Angela's gaze flicked over to me, and I didn't like the feeling of challenge I saw there.

"You think I'm going to cause a scene with my weak-ass magic?"

She blinked, her lips pinching up. I dropped my gaze before I said something else snarky.

Awkward silence filled the room, then Angela cleared her throat. "Are you feeling all right, love?"

I looked up, but she pressed her palm to Zo's forehead, talking to her, not me.

"I'm fine, just tired," Zo mumbled.

That was a safe answer since her mum had to have noticed the dark circles under her eyes. Angela paused, clearly wanting to ask more, but she didn't. She squeezed Zo's shoulder, instead, then headed out. She'd stopped trying to get answers about what happened at the school. From what the others had said, their families had given up asking too. I can't imagine what it would have been like for them, arriving to find the school half destroyed, the teachers having fled, and all of us shivering in the flooded wreckage. I know it must have been bad because when Zo told her parents I had nowhere else to go, her mum just hugged me and ushered me into the car.

Zo shuffled over in her chair, wrapping her arm around me and leaning her cheek against my shoulder.

"Happy birthday," she mumbled. The spiky ends of her short hair tickled my neck.

"Thanks." *So much for that being buried deep in my thoughts.*

"Toby was cross you didn't tell him."

I let out a half-laugh. "He didn't take the hint that meant I didn't want anyone to know?"

Zo shrugged, then yawned again, which set me off too. "Just accept that we love you and want to celebrate your birth."

I didn't know what to say. It's not like I'd had a long list of people "celebrating my birth" before. My dad used to send a card every year, when I lived with my grandma, but that stopped once I went into foster care. Not surprising, since I don't think he even knew where I was.

I stood, putting my bowl in the dishwasher and splashing some water on my face. "So, how exactly does one 'froof' cake?" I asked over my shoulder.

Zo made a "who knows" noise in her throat. "Probably the same way you zhush-it-up?"

"Helpful." I rolled my eyes. "Do you at least know how to make icing?"

"It's just butter and powdered sugar, right?" Zo stifled another yawn.

I could see at least ten ways that could go wrong if we messed up the quantities. Zo gave a sudden snort, making me jump.

"Finally!" she said.

"Huh?" I glanced back at her.

"Asher's up."

Already, the bags under her eyes had lightened with one less magical tie pulling her towards slumber. It wouldn't take long for Elijah and Julianna to wake now, their ties with Asher strongest. Honestly, it was amazing Toby managed to sleep in with both me and Zo up and chatting. I guess my nightmares had tired him out.

Zo stood, her movements far more energetic now. She grabbed a few things from the cupboard and started adding ingredients to the mixer. I cringed as she turned on the beater, sending the powdery sugar flying. She flung out a hand, and it froze, sparkling around us like fairy dust.

"Woah..." I laughed, and Zo stuck out her tongue, tasting the sweet air.

This is what I'd imagined magic would be like, before the school. The word "magical" had taken on a sinister meaning for me now, creating visions of killer plants and deadly dodgeball, but this is what it was supposed to be – sparkling sugar and fun.

Zo's breath hitched and she let out a massive sneeze, sending the sugar flying again. It scattered over the benches, landing as it would have if she'd never stopped it.

Zo rubbed her eyes and grinned. "Grab the vanilla for me, will you?" she said, as if nothing had happened.

I opened the cupboard, searching through the bottles of essences. Judging by the stickiness, they'd all been there a while. I checked the expiry dates.

Suddenly, everything swam in front of my eyes. I grabbed the shelf to keep myself upright.

Behind me, Zo stumbled too. "Callie!" She reached for me, and her fingers bit into my arm.

"It's okay, it's just Toby," I said.

Zo and I both blinked, clearing away the images of his bedroom, as he rubbed sleep from his eyes. Zo's hand relaxed on my arm, and I felt Toby smile as he found us waiting for him to wake up properly.

"Morning," I whispered.

Morning, came the reply in my head.

Zo rolled her eyes, but she laughed too, producing a few little sparks. "You two are so cute it makes me sick." She let off another round of giggle-sparks.

Of course, Zo's mum chose that moment to come back into the kitchen to grab her handbag. She dodged the sparks, and her frown deepened as she took in the scattered sugar. Her earlier words about not using magic echoed in my mind.

"You both look a lot more awake," she said, her voice tight.

Zo nodded. "Yeah, just like magic."

JOSH'S PARTY WAS ABOUT as exciting as you'd expect a ten-year-old's birthday to be. There were tears early on, and one kid with a sprained ankle, but mostly it was just watching them eat way too much junk food and hit each other with stuff. The most fun part was playing "guess which one throws up first" with Zo, though neither of us really wanted to win that particular game.

I reached out in my mind a couple of times, to see what Toby was doing, but he appeared to be singing the same song on repeat. Correction, he appeared to be singing the same three lines of a song on repeat. I did my best to block him out before it drove me nuts.

I was getting to the point of edging towards our bedroom, hoping Angela would consider my helping duties done, when I heard a car pull up outside.

"Finally!" Zo unfolded herself from the couch, getting up and stretching. "You have no idea how hard it's been to keep this a secret."

"Keep what a secret?"

She didn't answer, already making her way outside. I followed after her, mainly because I didn't want to be left in the house with 24 ten-year-olds, though I had to admit, she'd piqued my curiosity.

I stumbled in the corridor, as my vision swam. I saw the outside of the house through someone else's eyes. I blinked, trying to clear it. "Toby...?"

My heart started to flutter, and I picked up my pace, following after Zo. Before I knew it, I was running, a stupid grin spreading across my face.

Julianna stood on the lawn, leaning back into the car to get something. I dashed down the path, rushing straight into Toby's arms. He was only halfway out the car himself, and he stumbled back, not letting go of me.

"Oh my god, you're really here!"

Zo cracked up, letting off a ridiculous number of sparks. Julianna straightened up, and I reached out to her with my other arm. She and Zo piled on top, turning it into a teetering group hug.

"Ow, Zo!" Toby pushed her away and slapped a spark out of my hair before it caught flame. "Stop laughing, then you can hug us."

She laughed more in response. I pulled back to look at Toby, but I kept my hands on his arms, not ready to let go completely. His arms stayed resting around my waist.

I nodded to the car. "You got your license."

"Had to." Toby grinned. "How else was I going to get here for your birthday?"

My cheeks flushed, and delighted bubbles of warmth filled me.

He chuckled and gave me a little squeeze. "Happy birthday, Reactive Girl."

I'm sure my cheeks flamed at that. I ducked my head, letting my hair fall over my face.

"Elijah and Asher are on their way too," Zo told me.

Even though the two of them were the furthest away from me in the magical link chain, I could feel them coming closer, echoes of it passing through the minds of my classmates.

"It's so good to have you here," I told Julianna, though to be honest, of all my former classmates, she was probably the one I knew the least. My fault, since I'd yelled at her on my first day at the school. I mean, I *was* being kept prisoner at the time. That should give me at least a few free passes on angry behaviour.

She laughed. "And to think, you didn't want us to know when your birthday was!"

I frowned. "Yeah..."

Was it weird that she knew that? Sometimes I forgot the others were all much more interlinked than I was. Her connection with Zo probably meant she heard at least an echo of every conversation Zo and I had. I'd have to be careful what I said if everything got passed down the line like that.

Julianna's smile grew tense. I forced my frown into something more socially acceptable, trying to dispel the awkwardness, but I'm not sure I could ever entirely get away from resting-bitch-face. My default expressions were mild panic or surly scowl.

"Elijah and Asher might be a while," Zo said. "Let's head in. Mum's set up the basement for us."

Toby unwound his arms from around me. "Sounds good. As long as there's no possible-possums, right, Jules?"

Zo sent out another round of sparks, and Julianna's face went red. "It was dark!" She gave Toby's shoulder a playful shove.

"What's this?" I asked.

Toby shook his head. "Oh, nothing. Jules freaked everyone out last week, when she thought there was a possum in her neighbour's basement."

"It was their cat," Zo poked Julianna's shoulder, "which she's met."

"It. Was. Dark!" Julianna pouted, but a laugh broke through.

"Funny," I said, trying to keep my tone light.

Toby's eyes flicked to me, and his expression told me my attempt at playing it off hadn't landed. Apparently, my version of "light tone" was the vocal equivalent of resting-bitch-face. Not to mention he was probably reading my stupid jealousy in my thoughts.

Why did it bother me that they were all laughing about this? With their connections, of course there were going to be moments they'd all shared. Only some things filtered down to me, so I relied on Zo to tell me about it, or the glimpses I saw in Toby's head. I guess a silly story about a cat didn't rate as important enough to pass on.

I forced a laugh. "You should know, Zo's cat likes to attack feet. I've got the scratches on my toes to prove it."

"Oh god, not another one!" Julianna groaned melodramatically.

"That's how Loki shows affection," Zo said.

Toby scoffed. "What did you expect when you named your cat *Loki*?"

I let out a genuine laugh, this time, and Toby gave my shoulder another squeeze. His thoughts danced, pleased with himself at making me smile.

"Come on." Zo linked her arm through mine, then took Julianna's hand. "I promise I will protect you from all marsupials *and* felines."

I laughed, but it petered out as something caught my eye. A small sunflower had sprouted up in the middle of the lawn. I glanced at Toby, but he wasn't looking at me, still laughing with Zo and Julianna.

You're safe, I told myself. *We're all safe.*

But a little sunflower-shaped niggle made me have doubts.

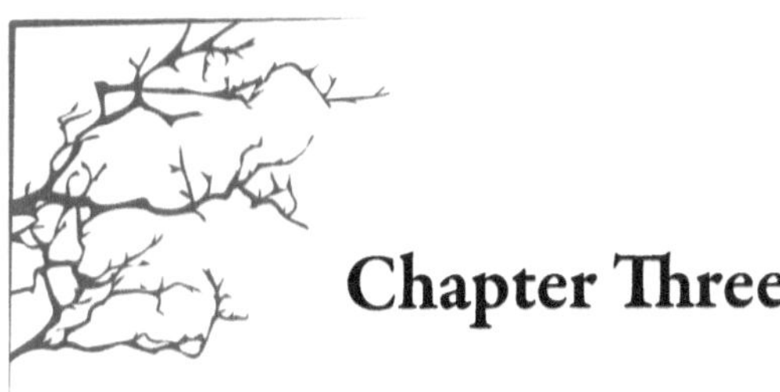

Chapter Three

Elijah and Asher arrived not long after that. A strange hum began pulsing in the air, as soon as they did, probably a magistation from Zo. At least it was less noticeable than the sparks – her mum would be happy about that. But it made a similar pulse start up behind my eyes, and the basement swayed in front of me.

None of the others seemed bothered by it. Of course, Asher only had eyes for Julianna anyway – big surprise there – and Elijah followed him around like a puppy. Asher tried to be nice, but honestly, I think he just wanted him to go away so he could focus on Julianna.

I don't know what it was about Elijah, but he'd always got on my nerves. I could only read Toby's thoughts, but I got the feeling everyone else felt the same. I'd overheard Zo calling him a sociopath, and Julianna hated him after he gave her poisonous flowers. We'd all changed a lot after Toby linked us, though, so I supposed I should give him the benefit of the doubt.

Really, I didn't care who else was here. I was just so happy to see Toby.

Zo's mum had set up the basement beautifully and gone to a lot of trouble with the food. She'd put as much effort into this as she had with Josh's party, which set a warm glow flickering in my stomach. I hadn't had a birthday party since I was a little kid.

"Good birthday surprise?" Asher asked me, finally dragging his eyes away from Julianna.

"The best."

Elijah scoffed. "Apparently you have low standards."

I frowned, and Asher rolled his eyes.

"Just be quiet, would you?" Julianna's tone was *almost* the same as the one she'd been using in teasing the rest of us, but there was an edge to it.

"What?" Elijah gave a stupid grin, which at the school had usually meant he was about to do something malicious. "You really think six people in a basement is anything other than lame? We're not even her friends, we're a bunch of losers she was held hostage with."

My stomach dropped. They were my friends, weren't they? Well, maybe not Elijah so much, or even really Julianna and Asher, but Toby and Zo definitely were... weren't they?

"Dude, shut up." Asher shook his head. "No more words, okay?" He grabbed a cupcake, shoving it in Elijah's mouth.

Julianna and Toby both laughed, but Elijah's face darkened. He glared at Julianna, wiping icing off his face, then he glanced down at the cupcake.

"This is pretty good," he said. He looked up, meeting Asher's eye. "Guess you did me a favour."

He always had this weird tone when he spoke, where I couldn't tell whether he was making a joke or a threat, no matter how innocuous his words were. He turned away, going to examine the food, and the rest of us let out a collective sigh of relief.

Though now the focus was off Elijah, it was back on me, and I didn't know what to do with myself. Toby took pity on me. He gave me a cupcake and pulled me over to the couch to sit down beside him.

"Thanks," I said, and I hoped he knew I meant not just for the cupcake, but for helping me behave like a normal human being in social situations.

"Sorry I couldn't get any of your old friends here," Zo said. "I had grand plans... but it kind of fell apart when I realised I had no idea how to contact them. I guess this *is* a bit lame."

I shook my head. "No, it's great. I love it." I didn't bother mentioning that *I* didn't have much idea how to contact my old friends. The school had gotten rid of my phone when they kidnapped me, so I didn't have anyone's numbers, and I couldn't exactly log on to my old social media without raising a whole bunch of questions about where I'd been for the last six months.

"She got the best people here, though, right?" Toby grinned. "Or should I say, best *person*."

Zo shoved his shoulder. He ruffled her hair up in response, and she let out an indignant squeal.

I felt awkward again. Was I supposed to join in the play-fighting? Basically the only fighting I'd done in my life was anything but play, though with Zo's magistations, even the lightest of roughhousing could quickly turn dangerous. I took a bite out of the cupcake instead.

Toby and Zo finally settled down. I couldn't tell who'd won; they both seemed to think they had. Zo glanced over at Julianna, and she went quiet, deflating. I followed her gaze. Elijah pestered Julianna and Asher again, and their patience was clearly wearing thin. There wasn't much we could do about that, though. There were only so many ways to tell the guy he was being a dick.

Zo frowned as she watched them. "I'm going to get some food," she said.

A light crackling filled the air, mixing with the pulsing hum – a magistation of her irritation at Elijah, I assumed. Not much we could do about that, either.

Toby flopped back on the couch next to me. Weirdly, now he was in front of me, I didn't know what to say. We'd been communicating in our heads for so long, it felt weird to speak aloud. Besides, the pulse drowned out my ability to think.

He stared at me for a moment, then his face broke into a grin. "I've missed you," he said.

I let out a breath. "Me too."

He wrapped his arm around me, and I settled against his shoulder. Zo put some music on, which instantly made things more comfortable. The beat hid her magistations and drowned out our conversation. Or it would have, if we'd ever started a conversation.

Something across the room drew Toby's attention. I glanced over. Julianna and Asher stood together, Julianna's head thrown back in laughter. They held hands, their fingers intertwining.

"So, they're properly together now?" I asked.

It wasn't a surprise. They'd been on the verge of it at the school, but with everything else going on, there hadn't exactly been time for a relationship to develop. I wondered if that might have been the only reason she was here – to get a chance to catch up with him.

"Yeah..."

Toby wasn't really listening to me. He frowned, his focus on Zo. She stood to the side of the room, chewing her lip. Her gaze kept travelling to Julianna and Asher, then she'd force it away, shaking her head as if chiding herself.

Elijah interrupted them, yet again, talking to Asher in an animated way. Asher nodded along, but his focus was clearly still on Julianna.

"I'm going to..." Toby trailed off as Zo turned and walked upstairs. A much louder crackling of static electricity filled the air, and I felt my hair frizz. Toby sighed.

I touched his arm, drawing his attention back to me. "What's going on?" I tried to read his thoughts, but they were scattered... half-formed. I felt his worry but couldn't quite see what it was attached to.

"Hm?" Toby glanced back at me, almost like he'd forgotten I was there. "Oh, nothing, Zo's just having a hard time with Julianna and Asher dating."

I frowned. "Why?"

Toby glanced at me, blinking. "She likes Jules. She didn't tell you?"

I shook my head, a little pit forming in my stomach. It was strange. Zo and I shared a room, so it felt like we were close... but we never really did the deep and meaningful conversations. Maybe she didn't feel like she could share stuff like that with me.

Toby shrugged. "To be fair, she never actually told me; I guessed. Can't you hear it in her thoughts, though?"

"I can only hear yours."

Sometimes I could hear echoes of Zo in Toby's mind, but not clearly. He was basically connected to everyone, all of their thoughts trickling along the line to him.

A flicker of a smile crossed his face, and he squeezed my hand. "Mine are the best ones though, right?"

Another warm bubble grew in my stomach. He chuckled, brushing the hair back from my face. For a moment, I thought he might kiss me, then he looked away, his eyes searching for Zo.

"I better go find her," he said. "Check she's okay."

I nodded. "Yeah, of course."

He squeezed my arm, then let go. "I'll be back soon."

I watched him walk up the stairs, feeling something I was horrified to find must be jealousy growing in my stomach. I didn't like how possessive I felt. The thread of magic joining us made me want to attach myself to him, but I had to remember he had those same magical ties to Zo.

I could understand why she was upset. With their connection, there would be no way for Zo to hide anything from Julianna. I couldn't imagine not only having unreciprocated feelings but knowing that the other person could see it all play out in your head. No wonder she ran away to hide.

If I was honest, I also felt sidelined by Zo. Why hadn't she told me she liked Julianna? Did she think I'd judge her? I wasn't exactly warm-and-cuddly best friend material, but I'd thought we were getting closer. Was that all in my mind?

I closed my eyes. *Toby will be back. He's being a good friend*, I told myself. Even so, the taut feeling of the magic thread between us niggled at me. Somehow it was worse when I knew he was so close but still out of my reach.

Raised voices made me look up. Elijah's conversation with Asher had devolved into an argument. I got up, wondering if I should run and get Toby. Julianna stood between Asher and Elijah, and leaving her alone seemed like a bad idea.

"Grow up!" Asher yelled at Elijah. "Stop following me around like a puppy."

Funny, that's exactly what I'd thought earlier. Perhaps the words had passed down the line, without me realising. I moved to stand beside Julianna.

Elijah scoffed. "You want me to stop following you? Let me off this bloody leash!" He flicked his hand, and the thread of magic joining him to Asher snapped tight. Asher stumbled, and the ripple of power jerked Julianna off her feet too. The pulsing in the air had turned from a hum to a deep bass. I covered my ears, disorientated.

"Quit it!" Asher shoved Elijah.

"Make me!"

Elijah moved as if to shove Asher back, but something glowed in his hands. Julianna dived forward, flinging her hand up. A fireball rose in the air, like the one Miss Trager had thrown at Toby. I froze, my stomach curdling at the memories. It floated in the air.

Julianna held her palm up, suspending it there. "What the hell, Elijah? Didn't you learn last time why we don't play with fire?"

Elijah sneered. "How about wind, then?" He threw his hands forward, sending the fireball crashing against the ceiling. Flames spewed out, lighting the room up.

Julianna and I both screamed. She rushed to put the flames out, but there were too many. Asher charged Elijah, abandoning magic for brute force.

"Stop!" I yelled.

Toby and Zo ran back into the room, but Elijah and Asher took no notice, clawing at each other.

"What the hell?" Zo tried to help Julianna with the flames, but they wouldn't go out, the energy from the fight feeding them.

Toby got between Asher and Elijah, and Elijah punched him, sending him stumbling back.

"Enough!" I shoved Elijah and Asher apart. The two of them flew back, landing on opposite sides of the room with a crash. Julianna and Toby were knocked off their feet too, and even I stumbled backwards. The house shook, the pulse bouncing around the room.

"The fire," Zo whispered.

As if in answer, water rained down on us, quenching the flames. I raised my face to it, letting it calm me. I had no idea if I caused the deluge, or if it came from one of the others. Either way, I welcomed it.

Stunned silence fell over the room, but the magic still bounced around us, sending plates and furniture crashing to the floor. I didn't know how to stop it. My heart raced, and I shook with the power of it, then suddenly Toby was beside me.

"It's okay, Callie, it's okay." He wrapped his arms around me.

"The kids," I whispered. A fire alarm screeched above us, and I could hear screams from upstairs. Adult voices shouted over the chaos, everything out of control.

Julianna ran to Asher's side, helping him up. Elijah laughed, his face plastered with that stupid grin. But I couldn't focus on either of them right now, not even to check whether they were all right. Zo's mum stood on the stairs. She took in the destruction, and I heard an echo of her earlier words in my mind. *You know there can't be any magic in front of the guests, right?*

Toby squeezed my shoulders, and I shivered as the cold water ran down my neck. I wanted to feel comfort in his hug, but all I could see was Zo's mum staring at me.

It wasn't my fault, I wanted to tell her. *I tried to stop them.* But she wouldn't believe me. Who would?

Finally, the rumbles of magic began to still, but the damage was already done. "I'm sorry, I'm so sorry," I said. "I didn't mean to do that."

"Sure you did." Elijah's voice sing-songed around his laughter. "Got a bit of a masochistic streak, haven't you?"

"Just shut up, Elijah!" Julianna screamed.

Elijah pulled himself to his feet. "Chill, Jules. Callie broke your boyfriend, not me."

She shook her head. "Just piss off."

Elijah smirked, though he walked stiffly from when I'd thrown him. "Can't with this around." He tugged on the magical thread, harder this time. I felt it ripple through the group, tugging from Asher, to Julianna, Zo, Toby then finally me. The world jolted with it. I wanted to jerk it back, flinging Elijah off his feet.

Julianna spun around, slamming her fists into Elijah's chest. "You ruin everything."

His face went dark. "By all means, blame everything on me. You always do."

Toby let go of me, moving in close in case he needed to step between Elijah and Julianna to protect her. But Elijah shook his head. He turned, pushing past Angela on the stairs and walking out.

For a moment, we just stood there, dripping in the water. It still rained down on us, and I didn't know how to make it stop.

"It's okay," Toby said, responding to my thoughts. He raised his hands, and the others all joined him, switching the water off with their magic.

Zo's mum cleared her throat. My eyes shot to her, and my heart gave a squeeze.

"I'll get a mop," she said, and turned, practically running up the stairs.

I sighed, sitting down on the damp couch and pulling my hands down my face. Toby joined me, wrapping his arm around my shoulder and saying comforting things. I ignored him. We didn't need a mop; we could easily clean up the water with magic. Or at least, my classmates could. Right now, though, we all just needed to breathe.

"Someone should go after him," Zo said. She made her way down the stairs, kicking through the puddles like she would start tap dancing.

We all waited for Asher to say he would, given he was the only one of us connected to Elijah. He stayed silent, his face flushed and jaw tightly clenched.

"I'll go," I said, surprising even myself. I stood up, before I could give myself a chance to back out.

Toby frowned. "You don't have to. It's your birth–"

"It's fine," I said, cutting him off. I followed Elijah's path up the stairs, not waiting for anyone to stop me.

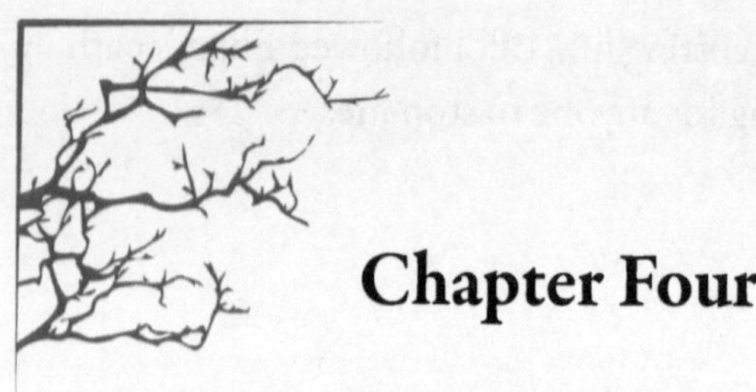

Chapter Four

I wandered down the street, looking for Elijah. I probably should have run to catch up with him, or at the very least broken into a light jog, but I dawdled. It wasn't like I had a clue what I would say once I found him. Volunteering to go after him had mainly been an excuse for me to leave.

I caught sight of him around the corner. He hadn't run that far. Perhaps he hadn't expected anyone to follow.

"Elijah!" I called.

His head jerked at the sound of my voice. He swayed on the spot, as if he might turn and run, but then he stilled, waiting for me. I made my way over to him. The pulsing hum intensified as I got closer. Strange – that must mean it wasn't one of Zo's magistations.

"Are you all right?" I wasn't sure whether I meant emotionally or from where I'd thrown him. He could interpret it whichever way he wanted.

He shook his head, and his face twisted. "I can't do this, okay? I just..."

I didn't need to be able to read his thoughts to know they were a swirling mix of anger and confusion.

"I hate this!" He tugged on the magical thread connecting him to the rest of us. The pull rippled through again, and I was jerked towards him, the force strong enough that I couldn't stop it.

I swallowed. I wasn't expecting this. He always behaved like such a cocky asshole; I didn't know what to do when I felt sorry for him.

His breathing slowed, and I found myself matching his inhales.

"All the time," he said quietly. "All the time, it's there, nagging at me. I want to be close to you all, but then I get here and…"

I reached out but stopped short of actually touching him. "I get it."

"Do you?" He sneered. "They all like you. Toby fucking loves you." He shook his head. "None of them like me. They're just bound to me, so they *have* to want me here."

"That's not true!" But even as I said it, I knew he would hear the waver in my voice. He'd behaved like a creep at the school – he'd given Julianna poisonous flowers and acted like it was funny, and thrown fireballs at me when I didn't have the magic to defend myself. I *did* want him here, but only because it eased the strain on the magical threads linking us. I didn't like him, and I couldn't tell him otherwise.

Elijah gave a half-laugh. "Yeah, exactly." He shrugged. "Don't worry, it's not like I give a shit about you either."

Strangely, that hurt more than I would have expected. I may not like him, but the bonds we'd all formed in saving each other's lives meant something to me. Clearly they didn't mean anything to him.

He must have read that on my face, because he shook his head. "See? I'm a jerk, you don't want me around."

I let the silence hang for a moment. I'd felt the same way for most of my life when I'd been in foster families. The families *wanted* to want me. They wanted to love me and be there for me, but it was always harder than they thought it would be. They'd found me prickly... too independent for them to bond with me.

I didn't know anything about Elijah's life before he came to the school. I didn't know much about his life now, for that matter. Maybe his situation hadn't been that different to mine, at least in the sense of feeling like an outsider.

I pulled gently on the magical thread and felt it ripple all the way through the others to Elijah, making him stumble a step towards me. He glared at me, but I shrugged.

"We're the ends, we've got to put up with being pulled around."

The hint of a smile played on his lips. "Maybe you get it a bit," he said quietly. He took another step towards me, watching my reaction.

The movement wasn't threatening, it was... something else. I wasn't used to people looking at me like that, and it sparked a little something inside me. He swallowed but didn't move away or break eye contact. Neither did I. His eyes were this really deep brown. On someone else they would have been warm, beautiful even. He took one more step towards me, and reached out, as if he would brush the hair back from my face.

The pulse grew stronger in the air between us, throbbing against my skull until I was sure my eardrums would burst. Heat flushed my cheeks, and I stepped back, wrapping my arms protectively around myself.

He frowned. "You feel that too, don't you?"

"Huh?" I forced myself to look back up at him.

"The magic pushes us away." He reached out again, and the pulse grew, vibrating until it hurt. His hand stopped, hovering near my cheek, almost as if he couldn't get any closer.

"Can't you feel that?" he asked.

The air turned thick between us, pushing us both back. It wasn't quite solid – we could have broken through if we'd wanted to – but the resistance was like pressing against the surface tension on jelly.

So that's why he'd moved so close to me. I shook my head. "I don't know," I said. "I don't always feel the magic."

He raised his eyebrows. "Wouldn't that be something?" He dropped his hand and looked away.

I wasn't sure why I lied. Something about this felt dangerous. I'd wanted so much to see everyone – I'd been so happy to have them all here, but was Elijah right? Was the magic trying to push us apart? I couldn't deny that something was happening, but maybe it had always been that way, and my magic hadn't been strong enough for me to recognise it. Had I ever touched Elijah before? Embarrassment rose inside me at the thought, and I was glad he couldn't read it. Maybe back at the school when we were trying to save everyone from Toby's siren plant. Everything had been so chaotic; I couldn't be sure.

Not for the first time, I wished my magic was simpler to use. Sure, it protected me when I desperately needed it, but the rest of the time it had a flat battery.

"I need some space," Elijah said finally. "Just leave me alone, okay?" He stepped backwards a few paces, then turned, walking away properly.

"Okay..." I mumbled, not knowing what else to say. "I'll see you later."

He raised his hand into a wave, without looking back. I watched him until he turned the corner, then let myself relax. I'd been holding so much tension, my limbs tingled now I'd let it go.

I took a deep breath, enjoying the freedom of being alone for one final moment.

Space.

It's what Elijah said he wanted, and it's what I'd been craving too. Slipping outside at night to stare at the stars helped, but it didn't stop the claustrophobic feeling of constantly being linked to five other people. It was a strange thing being desperate to be close to them, but also feeling trapped by it. We couldn't even choose when to sleep without the others all being affected by it.

I made my way back to the house, but stopped a couple of metres down the road, staring at the yard. The flower in the middle of the lawn had sprouted up, like an ornate yellow fountain in a green sea. It reached my ankles now, and smaller ones poked up through the grass in a couple of other spots. The crow I'd seen earlier hacked at them, sending a spray of mutilated yellow petals flying across the grass.

Could flowers grow this fast? I wasn't kidding myself that this was normal, but where were we on the continuum of strange-but-benign-magic to terrifying-siren-plant-trying-to-kill us?

Toby came outside, as I walked up the driveway. He spotted the sunflowers before he saw me, and he knelt down to examine them, a frown on his face.

"Hey," I said.

He glanced up, forcing the frown into a smile. Worry flittered behind it. His gaze travelled back to the sunflower, and the smile slipped.

"Are you okay?" I asked him. "Did I hurt you?"

Toby blinked. "What? No, that was amazing. You stopped everything."

I shook my head. "I don't think Zo's mum will see it that way."

"Nah, don't worry about it. Zo will explain what happened."

How many times had I heard something like that in one of my foster homes, only to find myself packing my bags the next day?

Toby rubbed his jaw. "Elijah on the other hand... He hit me pretty hard, you know?"

"Let me see?" I touched his face, running my hand over his jaw.

He swallowed, trying not to flinch under my touch. The pain of it echoed through his mind, and I felt the brush of my own fingertips on his skin, the sensation both fascinating and unnerving. We'd healed each other, once before – him saving me, me saving him. But like always, I couldn't control it.

Toby swallowed. I almost pulled away, but then his eyes flicked up to meet mine, holding my gaze.

"I know how he feels," I said. I wasn't sure where that came from; it seemed to burst from my lips.

Toby frowned. "Elijah?"

Heat filled my cheeks again at his name. Just moments ago, I'd been standing this close to him, and a pang of guilt hit me.

I wasn't sure what that was between me and Elijah, but I did know it shouldn't have happened. I shook my head to clear it.

"Me and him, we're on the edges," I said.

"What do you mean?" Toby ran his hand down the side of my face, mirroring the way I had traced his jaw. Again, I felt both the brush of his fingertips and the feel of my own skin under his hand. His thoughts, and my thoughts, simultaneously flicking through my mind.

"We talk about us all being connected, but we're not. You're joined to me, but also to Zo. Me and Elijah, we're the ends."

"But... we're all linked to each other," Toby said.

The way everyone's thoughts echoed down to him, I could almost have believed he was, but it was a horseshoe pattern. The missing link between me and Elijah broke the circle.

Toby had formed those connections to save us – to control our magic and stop it from destroying everything. And it had worked, we were safe. That didn't mean the magic was perfect, though.

"Except we're not. The magic is unbalanced. It's..." I didn't finish that thought, but I could see it pained him anyway. I hadn't been able to articulate this to Elijah, and I'm not sure it would have helped him even if I had.

I wasn't sure why Elijah and I weren't drawn to each other in the same way the others were. Instead, the magic seemed to want to push us away.

Toby didn't answer. I could see he was still confused and maybe a little hurt. I'd believed I'd been able to understand his thoughts, even with the distance we'd had between us. But he didn't know what I meant. How much had we been missing over the last few months?

He shook his head. "Aren't you connected to Zo too? You live with her... The two of you are friends."

I forced a smile, though I could tell there wasn't much warmth behind it. "The friendship helps, sure, but it's not the same as this." I tugged on the string of magic between us.

It pulled tight, and he stepped towards me almost without thinking. I swallowed. I wanted him to be closer. The threads of magic spiralled around us as if to cocoon us together. I wanted to melt into him, letting the magic join us until we wouldn't ever be able to separate. He tilted his head as if he were going to kiss me. I raised my face, moving my lips towards his.

His eyes flicked away. "Callie," he hissed.

His voice hit me like cold water. I stepped back. "I'm sorry, I–"

"No, look!" He grabbed my shoulders, turning me around.

One of the sunflowers had risen up, growing half a metre in the few minutes we'd been talking. It still grew now, giant petals writhing as they stretched out like the tongues of some godforsaken monster.

"It's like your siren plant, isn't it?" I covered my mouth, feeling ill at the memory. "I've created another one."

"No." Toby put his arm around me, rubbing my shoulder. "No... that was different. This is just..." He trailed off, unable to provide an explanation.

The leaves turned black, collapsing in on themselves as they began to wilt, and the stalk shrunk back down. It seemed to sigh as it shrivelled, its entire lifespan reduced to a single breath, until all that was left was a half-rotted pile of leaves and petals.

"I tried to create fire," I said, "and..." And then the man with the dog had scared me. None of that seemed like it should equate to this twisted mass of decomposing plant matter, but neither did anything Toby had done when he created the first one.

"Look." Toby released his arm from around me, to move towards the pile of mulch. He crouched down beside it. "It's dead now, see? It's not going to grow out of control."

I glanced around at the other flowers on the lawn. They withered in different stages of dying. Some, the petals were wilted, but others had dried out completely, becoming pot-pourri then crumpling and disintegrating to nothing.

Toby stood and took my hands. "You don't have to worry, Callie. The magic is safe now we're linked."

His expression was gentle and open. He genuinely believed that, and perhaps it was partly true. Even so, I pulled away from him. His face fell, and I looked down, embarrassment filling me. I didn't know why I'd done that. I'd wanted him to kiss me a minute ago – at least I thought I had – so why had I pulled away?

The silence hung for a moment, then Toby gestured to-wards the house. "We should head inside, I guess."

I nodded. "Yeah."

He hesitated, glancing down the road. "Is Elijah coming back?"

There was more behind that question. He'd seen what hap-pened.

I glanced down the street too, guilt filling me again. I knew Elijah wouldn't be there, but I stared as if he would appear. "He needed some time alone," I said, my voice tight. "Time to adjust to this. He's... confused."

I hoped Toby read the rest of that thought in my mind. I needed time too. Neither Elijah nor I were used to relying on other people.

"Okay... yeah, I can respect that." Toby stepped back a little, giving me space.

Suddenly, he seemed too far away, and I wanted to grab hold of him. His expression lightened, and I knew he'd read that in my mind. I shook my head, trying to clear it. I made myself take a step toward him, and he met me halfway. *This is okay,* I said to myself. *You're safe with Toby.* Another niggling doubt started in my mind though.

"The sunflowers..." I said.

He reached down, picking one of the plants which hadn't yet started collapsing in on itself. "They're just flowers, Callie, I promise."

He handed it to me, and I smiled at the yellow petals. In that moment, sunflowers were a happy thing again.

"Come on." He took my hand, intertwining his fingers through mine. "Let's go find the others."

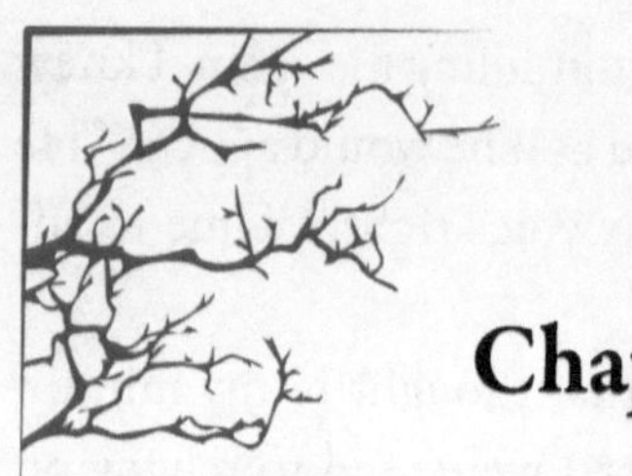

Chapter Five

I woke in the middle of the night. I wasn't aware of having a bad dream, but something had pulled me from the depths of sleep. Toby hadn't woken – I could feel the heaviness of his slumber from downstairs – and Julianna's slow breaths rumbled from the air mattress on the floor.

Zo had invited the others to stay the night. I think they'd all been ready to bail, but after getting some takeaways for dinner and watching a movie together, we all felt much more companionable.

Elijah came back halfway through the movie. A scowl twisted his face, of course, but we'd saved him some food and Asher caught him up on the movie. He'd seemed to soften after that.

The hum started up as soon as we were in the same room. I tried to ignore it, but I caught him staring at me a few times during the evening. He gave me a little smirk when I met his eye, and I was annoyed to find myself blushing again. Then I noticed Toby watching, and I'm sure I went from red to crimson under his gaze.

Finally, we'd all started to yawn, and decided to call it for the night. Zo's mum set the guys up to sleep in the basement, and Julianna joined me and Zo in our room. The gender divide was silly, given we'd all shared a room at the school, but I guess

Angela was still trying to pretend we were normal teenagers. Honestly, I was relieved. Things felt complicated with both Toby and Elijah now, and I don't think I would have gotten any sleep lying next to either of them.

I rubbed my eyes and yawned. My jaw clicked with the stretch. It had been a long day, but broken nights seemed to be a given now, even without confusing interactions with my male classmates. I glanced around at the familiar room, reassuring myself.

Zo sat bolt upright, startling me.

"You okay?" I asked her.

She didn't answer, perhaps still making sense of where she was. She sat perfectly still and straight-backed, as if this were a late-night attempt at yoga. A knot of anxiety formed in my stomach.

"Zo?" I propped myself up on my elbow to look at her.

Her eyes were wide and blank. She stared straight ahead, but she didn't seem to see anything. I swallowed, trying to ignore the goosebumps crawling over the back of my neck.

She moved suddenly, making me jump. She slid out of the bed, but then just stood beside it, staring at me with those blank eyes.

"Zo?" My mouth felt thick. "What are you doing?"

She turned, walking towards the door.

"Zo!" I scrambled out of bed. Julianna's mattress lay between me and the door, and I clambered over it, somehow not waking her. Zo disappeared into the hallway. "Where are you going?" I caught up to her at the top of the stairs and grabbed her arm.

She stopped, but her face remained blank. Voices came from Zo's parents' room, and I froze.

"You mean she just... threw them back across the room?"

My stomach dropped. Brian, Zo's dad, was talking about me.

"You said you asked them not to use magic today. They both promised they wouldn't!"

"Come on, Zo," I whispered. I didn't want to hear this, but more than that, I didn't want to get caught eavesdropping.

Angela had loudly insisted it was an earthquake, which most of the guests seemed to believe, but she'd been uneasy around me all afternoon. Evidently, Brian felt the same. I couldn't blame them – my whole life was an earthquake with me at the centre.

"You know they can't always control it." Angela's voice projected calm, and I felt a surge of warmth towards her.

"That's the problem! We've got five of these kids in our home right now. That doesn't scare you?"

"Of course it worries me, but Zo needs this. Besides, Callie's never used her magic here before."

"That's exactly why I'm afraid. If that's what it looks like, are we really comfortable having her here?"

My throat burned, and heat pricked the backs of my eyes. They were dry, though. I was used to this. I hadn't understood why in the past, but I'd always created chaos when I felt threatened. My foster families never blamed me outright – how could they when none of us had known magic was real? But it was never long until I was moved on anyway.

Zo turned towards the stairs. I clutched her arm again, but she spun towards me, shoving me with both palms. I stumbled backward, tripping and landing on my butt. Zo's mum and dad went quiet, the silence of them listening palpable.

Zo stared down at me. Her pupils were small, tiny black dots in the blue of her eyes. This wasn't sleepwalking. I hadn't seen her blink since she got up.

She turned away from me, making her way down the stairs to the front door. I heard someone get out of bed, though whether it was Angela or Brian, I wasn't sure. I dashed after Zo, not wanting to get caught by whoever it was.

Zo opened the front door and walked outside, in that same blank, almost robotic way. My heart danced against my ribcage, skipping and thudding to its own scattered rhythm. I stumbled across the threshold, my legs wobbly underneath me.

The front yard was empty, aside from the mess of shredded sunflowers the crow had distributed across the lawn. I glanced left and right, but there was no sign of Zo.

Where would I go if Brian kicked me out? I couldn't get rid of the tight feeling in my throat. A fleeting thought of Toby's family taking me in crossed my mind, and I almost laughed. I bet *his* mum would love that idea.

I shook my head, trying to focus. As if in response, a string of fireflies lit up, like they had that last day at school. I took a tentative step towards them, but then stopped.

I wasn't like the others. They had all known, or at least suspected, they had magic before being brought to the school. I'd still been convinced I didn't have any, even once I got there. My magic was always in the moment – Reactive, the headmaster had called it. It made it hard to trust – hard to be sure I was doing the right thing by following it. But right now, what other choice did I have? I broke into a run, following the path of lights.

The fireflies led around the corner, and I quickened my pace. My feet were bare, and I shivered in my pyjamas, but I kept moving. This felt like when Toby had followed me as I'd tried to find a way out of the school. It scared me to think that Zo might be trying to escape something too.

I caught sight of Zo up ahead. Her walk was unhurried but brisk, her steps as easy as if walking on a beach. Gravel cut into the souls of my feet, and I wondered how she didn't feel it. She wasn't searching for anything; she barely seemed conscious. It was almost like she was being puppeted.

She stopped suddenly, and just stood there, staring blankly in the middle of the road.

"Zo?" I called.

I approached her, slowly. She didn't react, neither running from me nor pushing me away. I reached out, looping my fingers around her wrist. Her arm remained limp under my grip, and the chill of her skin worried me. I pulled her towards the pavement. Her feet stayed planted, my tug only causing her head to tip towards her shoulder lifelessly.

"Come on!" My voice came out high and cracked. "You can't stay in the middle of the road."

"She can't hear you."

I spun around. Mr Grandace stood behind me. My breath caught, and I stepped instinctively in front of Zo, raising my hands as if I would produce a defensive spell. She didn't react. Her head slumped forward in a parody of sleep, but her eyes still stared, nightmarishly.

"What did you do to her?"

Mr Grandace had ditched the long cloak, and his devil-beard had grown out, taking on a softened shagginess, but he was no less imposing than the last time I'd seen him.

He raised his palms. "Peace, Calliope. I mean no harm."

I tensed, waiting for signs of him using magic on me, but there was nothing – no persuasion or manipulation behind his words, as far as I could tell.

"Zo is fine. I just wanted to talk to you, and I knew you would follow. I'll send her back if it would make you more comfortable." As if to prove his point, Mr Grandace flicked his hand, and Zo raised her head. She began walking slowly back towards the house.

For a moment, I wanted to run after her. To grab her hand, and hold her here, so I wasn't alone. Instead, I watched until she turned the corner, heading back towards home.

I lowered my hands, letting him believe he was in control of the situation, but I didn't relax my stance. "What do you want?"

He smiled. "Just to talk. That's all."

He had ripped me from my home and placed me in a school where my teacher tried to kill me. He'd kept me prisoner and put all of us in danger. There was nothing this man could say that I wanted to hear.

I swallowed. *Toby,* I said in my mind. I wasn't sure if he heard, or if he was even awake. My phone was back at the house. Mr Grandace could kill me right now, and no one would be any the wiser.

"You have no reason to trust me, I know that." Mr Grandace backed away a few paces, moving to sit on a low wall at the edge of one of the neighbour's properties. If he was trying to make himself seem less threatening, it wasn't working.

"Come, Callie, you can't stay in the middle of the road."

He never called me Callie – always my full name, Calliope. His manner seemed genuine – pleasant even – but everything he did was calculated. He watched me, as if curious as to what I would do.

He was right, it was stupid to continue standing in the middle of the road. I picked my way over the stray gravel to the pavement, keeping some distance between us.

Mr Grandace leaned his head back, looking at the stars. "It's beautiful, isn't it? Being able to see the sky. It was unfair of me to deprive you of this while you were at the school. I'm sorry for that."

That's what he was sorry for? Depriving me of the sky?

"What do you want?" I said again. It came out as a hiss.

Mr Grandace lowered his gaze, blinking as his eyes adjusted. "I want to tell you a story."

A strangled laugh escaped my lips, and I shook my head, my patience gone. "I'm not interested." I turned to walk back to the house.

"You should be. This affects you – all of you. You're not the first, you know."

Something in his voice made me stop and look back. He stood, the smile gone. The streetlight fell across his face creating dark shadows, and he seemed to have aged years in the last few minutes.

"The first what?" I cursed myself for asking that – for getting drawn in by him.

He swallowed and closed his eyes for a moment. "Reciprocus magicae – reactive magic. I told you it was a volatile combination for magic wielders to be both reactive and geminus pairs."

"But we're not geminus pairs. The magic is linked between all six of us."

The corners of his lips curled, but the smile it formed was tired. "In a way, yes. The six of you have created a… field of magic, for want of a better word. Within it, you draw each other in, your powers attracting each other's and growing stronger when they combine. We call it Magicae Magnes – magnetic magic."

In a strange way, that made sense. The thread of magic between us constantly pulled me toward Toby, but it wasn't just him. I wasn't connected to any of my other classmates, but I still felt drawn to them, like the pull of a magnet. All except Elijah. But even then, it fit. The magic pushed us apart, forcing us away from each other with that pulsing hum, like magnets of the wrong polarity repelling each other.

Mr Grandace studied my face. "In figuring out those links, you managed more than my six ever did."

I frowned. "Your six?"

"Like I said, you weren't the first, Calliope."

Toby had told me he'd thought there was something strange going on. The school said we were a pilot programme, but there was evidence the school had been around for a long time. We'd never considered that the headmaster might have been a part of that.

"What happened?"

"We were the first students of the school. Miss Trager and I are the survivors. The others…" Mr Grandace looked away, blinking slowly, the movement heavy. "They were destroyed by the magic."

Something jolted in my chest. I remembered the fearful way Miss Trager had introduced the subject of Geminus magic, the way she'd trailed off, barely able to bring herself to talk about it.

"Your magic is twinned with hers?" The two teachers seemed so different. But then again, my classmates and I had little in common outside of our magic. If the school hadn't brought us together, we may never have even met.

Mr Grandace shook his head. "Not me. Like your classmates, we were connected to others as well. We never understood that though. We thought we were three sets of geminus pairs."

I tried to imagine Miss Trager and Mr Grandace as teenagers, but I couldn't. They were both so imposing, it was hard to picture them as anything other than the adults who had terrified me the whole time I was at the school.

Mr Grandace cleared his throat. "When we realised the same pattern was going to happen again, we wanted to prevent... history repeating."

"Toby was the one who figured it out," I said.

Mr Grandace raised his eyebrows in question.

"*We* didn't figure it out. Toby did. He's the one who saved us."

Mr Grandace nodded. "That's true. Toby's connection to the rest of you is very strong."

"And Miss Trager tried to kill him."

Mr Grandace grimaced. "You have no idea how sorry I am about that."

I could almost believe him. I didn't think he had been a part of Miss Trager's plan – in fact, she had clearly done everything she could to keep him in the dark. It didn't absolve him. It was his fault we'd been trapped in the school in the first place.

He sighed. "Ursula... she lost more than the rest of us."

He didn't elaborate, but it didn't matter. He could make excuses for her all he wanted; I wasn't going to forgive her.

"Calliope, I understand why you're afraid to come back to the school, but–"

"No way." I moved away from him.

"You wouldn't be a prisoner this time, I promise." He took a step towards me. "It's not over, the magic is still unstable!"

"No!" I turned and walked away. I wanted to run, but I didn't want him to know I was afraid of him.

"Calliope!"

To his credit, he kept his distance. I knew this pattern, though; it's what he'd done when he first approached me about the school. He'd tried to convince me, tried to convince Lorna, my last foster mum, to send me to the school voluntarily. Then, when he hadn't got his way, he'd kidnapped me.

I could feel the others waking. It was amazing they'd slept through this far. Mr Grandace must have done something to them, in the same way he'd influenced Zo to sleepwalk.

I felt Toby making his way outside, searching for me.

"The magic is still unstable!" Mr Grandace called. "We thought things were normalising while you were apart, but the moment you came together–"

"Callie!" Toby's shout cut Mr Grandace off.

I couldn't see him in the dark, but I felt his magic pulling me in. I turned the corner, making my way towards it.

Pulling me in, just like a magnet. I shook the thought away.

Toby's arms wrapped around me. "What happened? Are you okay?"

"Let's get inside," I said.

Toby hesitated, glancing back towards where Mr Grandace had been. I saw it running through his mind – the idea of going after him, in some misguided belief that he could protect me. I grabbed his hand, pulling him towards the house.

Zo and Julianna stood in the doorway.

"What happened?" Zo asked.

I shook my head. Elijah and Asher watched us from the basement stairs. Five pairs of eyes stared at me now, but none of them had noticed Zo leave the house – Zo didn't even realise she'd been outside.

Toby locked the door behind us, and I leaned against him. He put his arms around me, and I could feel it; the pull of the magic, drawing me towards him.

We're safe. Mr Grandace is wrong. The magic is fine; it's sta-ble. But even as I thought it, I felt a niggle of something... a pulsing hum – the push of Elijah's magic against mine. Four strands of magic were pulling me in, while one of them tried to drive me away.

"WOW," ZO SAID, WHEN I finished telling them what had happened.

We'd congregated in the basement, hoping to avoid waking Zo's family. All was quiet upstairs when I got inside, and I didn't tell them what I'd overheard Brian saying. Still, his words circled around and around in my mind, fighting for precedence even over my conversation with Mr Grandace.

"UT and AG," Toby said quietly.

"Huh?"

He shook his head. "It's nothing, there was some graffiti on my desk at the school. The initials and a heart."

UT and AG – Ursula Trager and Arthur Grandace... it was strange to think about them like that.

"It's nonsense," Asher said. His jaw worked, making his words clipped and fast. "He just wants to get us back to the school. We're fine. Linking our magic fixed things."

Toby's hand found mine and squeezed it. I wanted to feel comfort in that gesture, but all I felt was the need to be closer to him. On the other side of him, Zo had shifted in tighter, and beside her, Julianna moved in too. All of us being drawn in together, exactly like a magnetic field. All of us, except for me and Elijah, the two ends, pushing each other away.

"It's not though, is it?" Julianna's voice was quiet, but we all dropped to silence as soon as she spoke. She glanced at Asher, and her lips twisted in a grimace. "We all felt it. Things started to go wrong as soon as we were together again."

Toby shifted uncomfortably. I could see it in his thoughts. He'd felt something wrong in the magic as soon as he'd arrived, but he hadn't wanted to acknowledge it. I looked around at the group and saw a similar discomfort on all of their faces. They'd all felt the same. It was so frustrating not being able to sense things in the same way they did. It was so hit and miss what magic I detected, and what went completely over my head.

Zo shook her head. "So, what's the solution? We never see each other again?"

Toby's hand tightened on mine, and Asher's arm around Julianna did the same. That couldn't be the answer, could it? Something squeezed in my chest. Never seeing Toby again felt like too great a punishment, not to mention the fact that I lived with Zo. Where would I go if I had to leave? Of course, I may not have a choice about that if Brian kicked me out.

"That can't be it," Toby said, his voice hoarse. "We made the magic better together."

Had we though? It's true we'd stopped our magic destroying everything by joining it, but it had only become dangerous because the six of us had come together in the first place.

Zo rested her head against Toby's shoulder, and Julianna touched Zo's arm. All of us drawing in yet again.

"Stop pussyfooting around it. We all know what the answer is." Elijah was the only one who didn't seem to be being pulled in tighter. He stood next to Asher, but they didn't make physical contact, Elijah's hands shoved deep in his pockets.

I frowned and he stared back at me, his face stony. My stomach started to tighten.

"Really, we don't," Toby said. I felt him glance at me, but I couldn't look at him. I squeezed his hand so hard, I was sure my nails must be biting into his flesh, but he returned my grip equally as tight.

"It's me and her," Elijah said, still staring at me. "We're the problem."

"We snapped the threads," I whispered. I remembered the feeling of it – the magic pulling tight, making it hard to breathe, and the pop as I broke them.

Elijah nodded. "And now we're the ones who need to leave."

Toby scoffed. "Don't be ridiculous, Callie doesn't need to go anywhere."

My throat felt clogged, but I forced myself to speak. "He's right." The thought of leaving Toby hurt, but the thought of him and the others being destroyed by the magic because of me hurt even more.

"No. He's not." Toby stood, still not letting go of my hand. "Just shut up, Elijah. You don't know what you're talking about."

I noticed the others were silent. They could feel it too – the push of magic Elijah and I caused. The rest of them were connected to each other – two people to help stabilize the power, and it worked... at least until Elijah and I threw off the balance.

Elijah sneered. "What, you think because you're into her, it's going to stop her getting all of us killed?"

Toby's face flushed, and he stepped towards Elijah. Zo and Asher stood too, getting between them, and Julianna moved to me, trying to comfort me or just getting out of the way, I wasn't sure.

"Calm down!" Zo's voice was a whispered hiss.

Asher put his hand on Elijah's shoulder, but Elijah flinched away. "Dude, just chill," Asher said quietly. I couldn't tell if it calmed Elijah or made him angrier. Either way, he turned his back on us, taking a deep breath.

"Mr Grandace is gone, right Callie?" Asher asked me.

I nodded. "I think so."

"Okay." Asher rubbed his chin, thinking. "So, we don't need to decide this tonight. I reckon we try to get some sleep now, and we talk it over in the morning when we're all thinking clearer."

Julianna moved back towards him. "I agree. That's a good plan."

I had to stop myself from rolling my eyes, but I nodded anyway. "Yeah, all right. We can try and sleep."

Zo jerked her head, in something that could have been a nod or a shake. "Yeah, whatever. I'm still creeped out that he made me sleepwalk." She moved towards the basement door but then hovered without opening it.

I felt Toby's eyes on me. I didn't want to look at him.

"Perhaps we should all stay down here," Asher said.

A collective sigh seemed to fill the room, and the others all murmured in agreement. Elijah scowled at me from across the room. I tried to ignore him. Everyone began rearranging blankets and pillows, as if any of us really thought we would be getting much rest.

Toby brushed the hair back from my face. "Promise me you'll wake me if anything else happens?" he said.

I forced myself to meet his gaze. "If anyone else goes sleepwalking, I promise I'll wake you this time," I said.

He studied my face for a moment, then nodded. He settled down in his bed, making room for me to join him. We'd shared a bed before – at the school, when neither of us felt safe enough to be alone. It still felt odd... way too intimate when I wasn't sure what we were to each other. If I was honest, it felt nice too.

I could feel Elijah's eyes on me, but I didn't look up. I lay down next to Toby, guilt brewing in my stomach. Technically, I hadn't lied to him. I didn't plan to be asleep when I went walking.

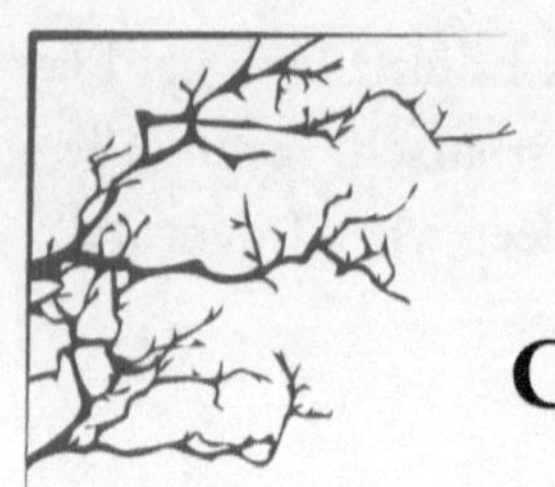

Chapter Six

It took forever for the others to fall asleep. Asher was the first, pulling Julianna down with him. Zo stayed up a little longer, her mind whirring with everything that had happened, but finally she succumbed to slumber. I thought Toby wouldn't be too long after her, but he resisted. Every so often, his restless limbs would flail as he tried not to drop off.

He kept looking over at me, but I stayed still and silent, hoping I would fool him into believing I was already asleep. Fat chance of that working when we were connected to each other.

I hummed a song in my head, using his trick of repeating the same three lines over and over to block out any other thoughts. After a while, his foot started to jiggle in time with the beat, and I couldn't help but laugh. I would miss being this in sync with another person.

Finally, I heard his breathing slow, and the tension on the thread between us eased as he dozed off. I waited, not daring to move in case I disturbed him, while straining against the pull of sleep. A part of me wanted to curl up next to him and close my eyes, but a couple of hours' rest wouldn't change things. We'd still be a danger to each other when I woke up.

I slipped out of bed, moving carefully. There was something calming about listening to all of them breathe, their exhales heavy. Toby's lips parted as his jaw relaxed, the softness making him look younger. I brushed his fringe back from his face and leaned down to kiss his forehead.

"I'm sorry," I whispered.

And then I left, before I had a chance to change my mind.

I didn't really have a plan. *Get away from the others*, was about as far as I had gotten. The question of where I could go swum in my mind – not just where I could go tonight, but where I would live. Zo's family had taken me in when I had nowhere. Being alone again terrified me.

I got changed quickly, grabbing my phone and a few spare clothes from upstairs. I shoved them into a bag, then slipped out of the house.

I only made it a few steps before the smell of rotting plants made me reel back. Layers of decomposing sunflowers littered the lawn, and a few live ones poked up between the mess. They had to be multiplying by the minute. Toby could tell me this wasn't like his siren plant all he wanted, but he couldn't convince me this wasn't dangerous.

I shivered in the night air. The live sunflowers turned towards me, their faces watching as if they would grow legs and follow. I picked my way through the mulch and out onto the street.

I SCANNED THE TIMETABLE fixed to the wall of the bus station. Even if I didn't know the destination, getting out of town seemed the best way to ensure my magic didn't hurt anyone, myself included. There was only one more bus leaving tonight, heading to Hamilton. I blinked at the name, wondering if it was a sign. Hamilton was where my foster mum lived, where *I'd* lived, until Mr Grandace had forced me away to the school.

The bus left in a few minutes. I made my way to the ticket office, but a sudden, horrible realisation hit me. I'd left my wallet at Zo's. An even worse realisation followed quickly after, that I probably didn't have enough cash in it for the fare anyway. Zo's parents had given me a credit card for emergencies, but I couldn't exactly use that while running away.

I sat down, laying my head in my hands. Dampness crept through my jeans from the bench, and that seemed about right for how this night was going. The thread between me and Toby strained with the distance, even though he hadn't woken. It brought with it the taut sensation that had pulled at me all the time we'd been apart. It would be so much easier to go back, even if we did get hurt because of it.

"Thought the idea was to get away from each other."

I jumped, scrambling up from my seat. Elijah stood in front of me, his face in a stupid smirk. His eyes travelled over me in a way that made me want to squirm.

I stared back at him, scowling. "What are you doing here?"

He shrugged. "Same thing you are, I'm guessing."

"Kind of defeats the purpose, if you're here." I shifted my weight, eyeing him.

He gave a half-laugh. "That it does."

He didn't walk away, though. Strangely, he seemed more relaxed around me now. The pulsing hum rose, but weaker this time, almost indistinguishable from my own heartbeat. Perhaps we didn't repel each other as much without the rest of our classmates pulling us in different directions. Or maybe we were getting used to the effect it had on us.

He nodded at the timetable. "You heading to Hamilton?" he asked.

"I was, but I forgot my wallet." I didn't mention the non-existent funds inside it.

He scoffed. "Ever heard of magic, Callie? Oh wait, that's right; you're useless at that."

I frowned. "Saved your ass from Toby's plant, didn't I?"

He smirked, then walked over to the ticket office. I followed him, more out of curiosity than anything else. The woman behind the counter looked tired, and I almost wanted to warn her that Elijah was doing something dodgy. Would she get in trouble later, if her supervisor found out she'd given us tickets without paying?

I watched what he was doing, intrigued, but knowing I wouldn't be able to replicate it myself. Elijah and Asher's powers had always been the strongest in the group, and I had to admit, it was fascinating to watch them in action.

In movies, characters always presented a napkin or old piece of paper in these situations, tricking the person into believing it was money. But as Toby had told me a few times, pretty much everything we'd ever seen or read about magic was wrong.

Instead, Elijah just talked to the woman. I'm sure if I'd been able to see things in the way that Toby did, I'd have seen clouds of colour spilling out from him, magical persuasion calming and confusing her. After a minute, her eyes glazed over, and she swayed on the spot. She took two tickets out of the drawer and handed them over.

Elijah grinned, but then stifled it. I glanced around at the other people at the station. Most of them were drunk or out of it – the usual crowd at this time of night – and none of them were in the best state to be noticing magical goings-on.

Elijah thanked the woman, then made his way over to me, the grin morphing back into a smirk.

"Will she be all right?" I wondered if the woman would be handing out free tickets all night.

Elijah frowned. "She'll live."

I didn't need to be connected to him to feel his irritation at my lack of admiration and praise. To be fair, I probably should have at least said thank you, but I wasn't going to congratulate him for brainwashing some poor stranger.

He handed me the ticket. His fingers brushed mine, and his hand lingered longer than it needed to. The magnetic push built up, but for some reason, neither of us moved away.

I swallowed, stepping back. I stared at the woman behind the counter, then at the ticket, then the ground – anything to avoid looking at him.

Elijah studied my face for a moment, and the hum grew in the silence. He turned away, heading towards the bus. I let out a breath and shook my head.

"Wait up!" I broke into a jog, following after him.

He didn't look back, but he slowed his pace, letting me catch up.

"WHY HAMILTON?" I ASKED him, once we were on the road.

The pulsing hum pressed against us, intensifying the bouncing of the bus's wheels. Empty seats surrounded us, only half a dozen other passengers on board. Under different circumstances, I might have sat alone, but a creepy dude with long, greasy hair sat a couple of rows away, staring at me, and Elijah seemed like the safer option. Besides, after a while, the hum quieted down to a manageable level, as if growing bored with trying to force us apart when neither of us were listening.

He shrugged. "Last bus leaving tonight."

I didn't think that was the whole truth. I was certain he'd followed me here. Strangely though, I wasn't mad about it. We'd both decided we needed to get away from our classmates, only to find we weren't quite ready to fully leave each other.

"They're going to be pissed you left." Elijah's smirk returned.

"Yeah." More than pissed, Toby would be hurt. We'd survived the school by sticking together, but if our magic caused damage every time we got close...

"Don't worry about it. We're the type who do better on our own, anyway." Elijah settled back in his seat and closed his eyes.

The rhythm of the road underneath us jolted my head against the seat, this time countering the hum I felt from Elijah. I wasn't sure how I felt about him saying we were the same. Sure, we'd both been loners before we came to the school, but Elijah was the type of loner who poisoned his classmate as a joke. For me, it had always been part choice, part circumstance.

Something twisted in my stomach. I'd thought that in the past tense. I had been a loner, but Zo and Toby had become my best friends... maybe even something more in Toby's case. I cared about Zo's family, and Julianna and Asher were important to me too. Even Elijah had become like a weird cousin.

I shook my head. It didn't matter. In six hours, we'd get off this bus, and I'd never see any of them again.

I tried to relax back in the seat, but my muscles clung to the tension. I felt like a meerkat, constantly on alert, looking out for threats. Whether I thought they were going to come from the other oddball passengers, or from Mr Grandace, I wasn't sure. A part of me even expected Toby to appear, though how he would do that with the bus moving, I don't know. I resisted the urge to reach out to read his thoughts.

"I guess it won't be long before they realise we're gone," I said.

Elijah shook his head. "We'll be fine. I deepened their sleep. Won't work on Asher for long, but Toby and Zo are weak."

I stared at him. After what had happened with Mr Grandace, I didn't like the idea of him messing with our friends' sleep.

He rolled his eyes. "Don't look at me like that. I do it on myself all the time. How else would I get any rest with you losers talking all night?"

"Fair enough." I had to admit, it would make things easier. At the very least, it meant I could stop singing the same stupid song over and over. Of course, now it was stuck in my head.

"So why Hamilton for you?" Elijah asked.

"It's where I used to live. I thought maybe Lorna, my old foster mum, would take me in."

"Good luck with that." He smirked.

I rolled my eyes. "Thanks."

"Why were you in foster care?"

I looked up, surprised. It had been a long time since anyone asked me about that. I'd told Toby and Zo the whole thing a while back, but I didn't think the others would be interested. The way Elijah asked the question, it was like he hadn't known that was a part of my history. Why did he think I lived at Zo's?

He held my eye, his face neutral... no hint of the usual smirk or scowl. His expression wasn't exactly warm, but there was something soft about it when he wasn't pulling faces. It made me want to at least try to trust him.

"I lived with my grandma when I was a kid, but then she died. There wasn't anyone else."

A depressing story, but not the worst I'd heard by far. The only really rough part was that I was old enough and surly enough that the chances of me being adopted had been slim to none.

He frowned. "What happened to your parents?"

"My mum died when I was born," I told him, keeping it simple. "My dad... I guess he wasn't very good at being a dad."

Elijah's expression was serious for a moment, then his lip quirked into something mean. "That's a lot of dead people around you. You sure you're not killing them off?"

"You're an ass." I turned my face away, staring out of the window. It was too dark to see anything, the light from inside the bus turning it into a mirror. I watched Elijah in the reflection. His eyes fluttered, regret filling his dark eyes. I didn't care. He could sit with that guilt. I would have changed seats, if it wasn't for the fact I'd have to climb over him to do it.

Elijah fell quiet, then he cleared his throat. "My sister's adopted," he volunteered. "Her birth parents died too."

"Good for you."

I waited for the joke – something about us both being killers, or both freaks... a cheap laugh where he could make me feel crap about myself. Instead, he settled back in his seat, closing his eyes again. This time he didn't reopen them.

I HALF WOKE AS THE bus pulled into the station. My head lay on Elijah's shoulder, the bare skin of his neck warm against mine.

"Cal?" he whispered. He touched my face gently, his thumb caressing my cheek.

I opened my eyes, startled. He held my gaze for a moment, his expression soft, then a wave of magic slammed into both of us, ricocheting around my head. I groaned, pulling away from him. The pulsing hum eased as I did.

He cleared his throat. "You were drooling on me," he said.

"Yeah?" I asked, but he was already on his feet. He didn't look back at me before disembarking and heading off into the night. I guess we weren't going to bother with any awkward goodbyes.

I watched him go. He was the resourceful type – too smart for his own good, Lorna would have said. Besides, he knew how to use his magic to his advantage. Still, I wondered where he planned on going. Did he even have a plan?

He was gone by the time I got off the bus. I stood for a moment, half waiting for him to reappear, then I made my way to the street. It had been a while, but I knew these roads better than anywhere else. Lorna lived about a 45-minute walk from the station, but that was fine. I set off at a steady pace.

The sun peeked over the hills in the distance, turning the sky a yellowy grey. I didn't want to wake Lorna – she'd be more amenable to hearing me out and letting me stay if she'd had enough sleep. Besides, I didn't know who she had with her now. She might have taken in another foster kid, if my disappearance hadn't put her off. My stomach twisted at the thought, but I shook my head. I would cross that bridge when I came to it.

I'd gotten soft living at Zo's, not having to walk anywhere. By the time I turned into Lorna's street, a raw, burst blister rubbed against the heel of my shoe, and my thighs ached.

I'd been intending to hang around outside until it got to a decent hour, but a yellow glow spilled out from Lorna's front windows onto the grass. Strange. Lorna normally struggled to get up early, sitting in the dark with her coffee for ages before she could open her eyes properly.

I hesitated, a tight feeling building in my stomach. Had Zo's mum called her to say I was missing? No, that couldn't be it. I'd told Toby and Zo about Lorna, but they wouldn't know how to contact her.

I shook my head. I was being silly. It had been months since I'd seen her – perhaps she'd taken up a health kick, getting into early starts. I crossed the road, heading over to her house.

The lawn sprouted up in overgrown tufts, but the flowerbeds sat in regimented rows, all neatly weeded. It made me laugh. Lorna would never admit it to anyone else, but the lawnmower terrified her. She was convinced one day she'd accidentally run over her foot and lose all her toes. I'd taken over the gardening after she told me, but I still teased her about it every week.

I took a breath, then knocked. A rustling came from inside, then Lorna opened the door. I wanted to explain straight off – give her the whole spiel about how I hadn't really run away; Mr Grandace had kidnapped me, and I'd never wanted to leave her.

The words died on my tongue. Her eyes widened as they fell on me, and she frowned, almost as if it took her a moment to place me.

"Callie," she whispered.

"I'm sorry," was all I managed to say.

She stepped forward, wrapping her arms around me. I started to cry, relief and exhaustion overwhelming me.

She turned her head, as if to kiss my cheek, but instead her lips moved to my ear. "Run!" she hissed.

I froze. Her hair covered my face, but I opened my eyes, sensing movement behind her.

"Go!" Lorna shoved me out of the house, and I stumbled back.

"Lorna..."

"Just run, Callie!" Lorna slammed the door in my face. Through the frosted glass panel, her blurry image turned to face someone – someone with long blonde hair. Miss Trager.

"No!" I clawed at the doorknob, then slammed my hand against the glass.

Both blurry figures turned towards me. Finally, my brain kicked in. If Miss Trager was here, it was for me not Lorna. I stumbled backward, breaking into a run. Behind me, the door opened but I didn't look back. What was she doing here? Had she known I would come?

It didn't matter; I had to get her away from Lorna. My head pounded, and my feet slapped against the pavement. I didn't dare look back. I might be able to outrun her, but her magic far outweighed mine.

"Calliope..."

Her voice whispered into a hiss, but it echoed around me. Underneath it, a slithering sound, like thousands of crawling insects crept across the ground towards me. And behind that, static, like a radio tuned to nothing.

Something wrapped around my ankle. I stumbled forward, somehow keeping my feet under me. I turned back, kicking, trying to free myself. Vines spread across the pavement, stretching out to grab me. I screamed and ripped the vine off my ankle. It disintegrated as soon as I touched it, but more reached out, sliding over each other like a pit of snakes. I scrambled away, then broke into a run. Were the plants real, or was Miss Trager manipulating me, making me see something she knew I would be afraid of?

Vines crept up from between cracks in the pavement in front of me. The slithering hissed in my ears, magic and reality blurring. I couldn't tell which way to run.

She appeared on the road in front of me, blonde hair strewn over her face, swirling in the wind as if alive. I turned, stumbling back towards the mess of creepers.

They parted, a gaping hole opening in the middle ready to swallow me. I froze, and the vines seemed to as well. Time slowed as they closed in on me. Feelers stretched out like forked tongues eager for a taste of my flesh.

A battered, rust-covered car pulled up in front of me. The door swung open.

"Get in!" Miss Trager sat in the driver's seat.

"Wh-what?" I turned. The blonde lady who'd chased me stood, still behind me, her hair falling over her shoulders now. She sneered at me, her face familiar but not. Not Miss Trager, at least.

Elijah's head appeared from the backseat. "Just get in the car, Callie!"

"Elijah? Why–?"

"We don't have time for this, get in!" Elijah grabbed my arm, pulling me into the car beside him. The tyres squealed as Miss Trager floored it.

The force flung me back against the seat. "I don't understand," I said. My head filled with the hum of being too close to Elijah.

We lurched around a corner, sending me crashing against him. He cursed under his breath, the pulse pounding in both our heads. He leaned over me to yank my seatbelt out. "Explanations later. Escape now."

I took the seatbelt from him, but didn't buckle myself in. "Seriously, what the hell?"

Miss Trager didn't glance back at me. Her eyes moved to the rear-view mirror, looking at the road behind us. She swore, hitting the accelerator.

I clutched my head as the slithering turned to a hiss. The vines were outside the car; it shouldn't have been this loud, but my ears rang with the noise.

Suddenly, she slammed on the brakes, throwing us forward. She spun the wheel to the right, sending me flying across the seat towards Elijah. He grabbed my arm, but the force of the magic between us threw me back. I gasped, trying to get air in my lungs.

My head rang, overloaded with the sounds of that pulsing hum, the static, and the slithering vines. "How is she still chasing us?"

Miss Trager shook her head. "No, it's not her." Her face paled, and her hands gripped the wheel so tight all the tendons popped up on the backs of her hands.

The car made a strange chugging sound, and our pace slowed to a crawl.

Miss Trager swore under her breath. I turned to Elijah, hoping to make an escape plan, but he stared horrified at the window beside me. Vines covered it, layer after layer of leaves slithering over each other. One crept through the gap in the window beside Elijah, reaching out to graze his cheek.

"Shut it! Shut the window!" I screamed.

Elijah scrambled for the switch, but the vine circled his neck. I wrenched it away. Heat pulsed through my palm and the leaves disintegrated. The car ground to a stop, and more vines crept up over us. Between them, a man walked towards us. It was him – the man I'd seen with the Labrador outside Zo's house. He held my eye, his pace unhurried as he stepped towards us.

"Callie!" Elijah yanked a vine away from me. "Snap out of it!"

The vine turned on him, wrapping around his wrist instead. Another tightened around my leg.

I blinked. The mess of leaves covering the car hid the man from view and blocked the light from outside. Elijah hit the overhead light switch, gifting us with a weak orange glow. The vines grew towards it, climbing up our bodies as if they would smother us.

Miss Trager rummaged in the dashboard compartment. She undid her seatbelt. "I'm sorry, Callie," she said.

"Wait, what?!"

She reached over the back of the seat, grabbing my wrist and shoving a silver bracelet onto it.

"No!"

She started to climb over the seat, reaching for Elijah, and I threw myself in front of him to block her. The force of the magic shoved me away. I crashed into Miss Trager, and she screamed as her back hit the dashboard.

I scrambled for the door handle, ready to face whatever was out there over becoming a prisoner again.

Miss Trager grabbed my other wrist, shackling it. "It's the only way, I'm sorry!"

Elijah yelled something, but his words crackled with static. Miss Trager opened the car door, squeezing her way out between the vines. They piled into the car, ignoring her. She walked towards the man, another pair of those silver bracelets in her hand, as the vines constricted around my chest.

I tried to scream, but my body disappeared beneath me. I reached for Elijah's hand, and I saw him reach for mine, but our fingers slipped straight through each other's.

Chapter Seven

I shivered. Cold floor pressed against my cheek, and darkness surrounded me. I eased myself up. My shoulder clicked, stiff from lying in an awkward position, and hot pain told me bruises lined my hip.

"Elijah?!" I called. My voice bounced back to me.

I scanned the room. The narrow width indicated it was a corridor, but other than a few framed photographs, the white walls and wooden floors were plain, nondescript. It didn't matter – I knew I'd been sent back to the school. I'd known the moment Miss Trager slapped those bracelets on my wrists.

A vine clung to my arm, tiny burrs attaching it to my sleeve. I threw it off, afraid it would come alive again. It disintegrated as soon as it hit the floor, more magic than plant.

"Elijah?" I called again. Had she sent him with me, or had she left him to his fate with the vines and whoever that was outside the car?

I closed my eyes, reaching out in my mind. *Toby?* I whispered. *Please... I need you.*

Nothing but the sound of static responded. Elijah's sleep spell must still have Toby in its grip. A shuddering breath broke through my lips, and I cried, indulgent self-pitying tears. How could I have been so stupid as to try to shut him out? The melody of the song I'd been singing echoed in my head as if to mock me.

I lay back down, giving in to the exhaustion. Something niggled at my mind, a little sensation at first, like an itch in my brain. The static came in waves, almost like words trying to break through, then the itch became a pull, making me dizzy each time I didn't follow it.

"Toby?" I sat up. The static surged as I did. I stood, letting the pull make my body sway forward. I took a few hesitant steps then broke into a run.

The corridor ended at a glass firestop door. Beyond it, stairs led into shadow. I tried the handle. The locked metal tooth jolted against the frame keeping me firmly out.

"Toby?" I knocked, then banged on the wooden frame with the flat of my hand. "Toby, please!"

I peered down the stairs, but darkness covered everything. He had to be down there. He was the only person whose magic drew me in like that, but why wasn't he answering? A sick feeling clogged my throat. What if he was hurt? I'd left him – left all of them – with those sunflowers growing outside. I thought the danger was in all of us being together, but what if I'd left them to a worse fate? If the sunflowers attacked like the vines, there would have been no way for them to get out of the house.

I leaned my head against the door, reaching out with my mind. Nothing but static replied. Did that mean he was unconscious?

I swallowed and tore myself away. I was no use to Toby just standing there.

I turned the corner, into the next corridor. I didn't recognise the hallway or the rooms flowing off it, though that didn't surprise me. Most of the areas of the school we'd spent time in had been destroyed by Toby's plant.

I stopped, suddenly. Darkness shaded my vision, but I could just make out the shape of someone lying on the floor in front of me.

"Toby?" I whispered.

The figure groaned, raising a hand to rub his face. Light glinted off a silver bracelet, circling his wrist.

"Elijah!" I raced towards him, but the familiar pulsing hum and wave of nausea hit me. I forced my way through it, grabbing his shoulder.

"Wake up! Please just wake up."

He groaned again and opened his eyes. Immediately his magic hit us both like a slap. I scooted back, clutching my head and feeling my stomach turn.

Elijah rolled over, looking like he was going to be sick. "Jesus, Callie. I know I'm irresistible, but..."

I broke into a sudden, high-pitched laugh. He sat up, and I shuffled back further. The nausea subsided as I did.

"Are you okay?" I asked. "Are you hurt?"

He shook his head. "Nah, I'm all right."

He didn't ask if I was okay, but that wasn't exactly unexpected. We'd never been friends, even before we became magnetically opposed.

He eased himself into a sitting position. "Where are we?" He touched one of the bracelets on his wrist, frowning at it.

"The school." I stood, walking away from him. "I think Toby's back here. I can feel his magic, but the door's locked."

The pull still called me. I moved towards it, and waves of static washed over me.

Toby? I called again. Silence greeted me. *Was* it him? No one else's magic had ever drawn me in like this. But that static... it felt like a warning. Elijah stood, leaning against the wall for support.

"I don't recognise this." He moved to look in one of the rooms, leading off the corridor.

"No..." I made my way back towards the stairs, the pull of magic drawing me along. "We destroyed so much of the school. We must be in staff quarters or... it doesn't matter, can you just help me?" I reached the glass door and rattled the doorknob again. "Between the two of us, we can probably get him out."

"Cal..."

I turned, looking back at Elijah. He stared at me, a frown creasing his forehead.

"That's not..." He hesitated, seeming to read something in the air. "I don't know what you're feeling, but your boyfriend's not here."

"But..." I reached out again in my mind. Toby's voice didn't greet me, only that pull.

Elijah watched me, his expression hard to read. I had a feeling he was waiting to see if I'd rise to his "boyfriend" comment, but this wasn't the time for games. I rattled the door handle one more time, as if something might have changed in the last few seconds.

Elijah took a step away. "My magic's stronger than yours," he said quietly, "and I'm telling you, none of the others are here. It's just us."

"Then what is that?"

Elijah stared through the glass. I could tell he felt it too. His body swayed, as if he wanted to give in and walk towards it, then he shook his head.

"I don't know," he said finally. "But if it's trying that hard to get us to walk towards it…"

He turned, walking the other way. I was torn. The pull of magic crept around me, seductively. Maybe Elijah was wrong. Maybe Toby lay on the other side of that door, waiting for me to find him.

I shook myself. Or maybe it was another siren plant. I took one last look through the door, then ran to catch up with Elijah.

I stayed a few paces back, keeping enough distance so our magic didn't interact. He tried the door handles as he passed them. Most were locked, and the only one that opened led to a cupboard.

I matched his slow pace, still keeping my distance. "How did you end up in the car with Miss Trager?" I asked.

Elijah blinked, as if he'd forgotten that even happened. "Same as you, pretty much. I was walking, trying to figure out where to go, then this guy appeared and started throwing plants at me."

"A guy? Did he have a dog?" I asked, thinking of the man outside Zo's house.

Elijah frowned. "What? No."

"But was it the same man who covered the car in vines?"

"Maybe? I don't know, I couldn't see through the leaves."

It was all so confusing. Who were those people, and why had they attacked? Even more puzzling was the fact that Miss

Trager had been the one to save us. But why had she sent us back here alone?

Some instinct made me look down. I froze. "Elijah, stop!"

To his credit, he listened. He halted, midway through a step, and turned back towards me slowly.

"There's a rune line."

"So?" He shook his head. He'd never seen what had happened to me when I crossed the runes while trying to escape the school last time.

I held up my wrist, gesturing to the bracelet. "You can't cross the lines with these on. They'll bind you in place." In the past, they'd also alerted the headmaster to the fact that I was trying to escape. I had no idea if they would do that now – I had no idea if Mr Grandace was even here.

Elijah sighed. Magic trapped us – rune lines in one direction, and some type of siren in the other. He shrugged, then turned around. We made the same slow progress back down the corridor, trying the doors on the other side.

"Why do you think they're coming after us?" I asked. "That man was outside Zo's house – the night before this all started."

Was that yesterday? I was losing track of the days. So much had happened in such a short space of time. I'd gotten used to the peaceful nothingness of living at Zo's. Sure, I'd been missing Toby and the others, but at least life had been calm.

"I don't know." Elijah didn't seem that interested. He focused on rattling the door handles, trying to get one to open. It was silly at this point, and the noise got on my nerves.

I glanced around at the unfamiliar walls. "We're on the other side of the lines," I said. Was that the rune line I'd crossed to distract Miss Trager from finding Toby? The dim light made it hard to tell.

At the time, I'd thought the runes were about keeping me from escaping, but maybe there was more to it. Maybe they also hid something on this side of them.

Elijah tried another door, and it creaked open. He grinned at me, then flicked on the light switch inside. The room lit up, a warm glow spilling out into the hallway. Elijah's eyes scanned the room, until his gaze caught on something. "Woah," he said.

"What's in there?" I asked.

He didn't answer, instead moving into the room, creating enough space that I could join him.

The room was a bedroom, but not like the one we'd slept in when we lived here. Ours had never lost the sense of temporariness that came with our boarder status. This room had been lived in – had grown up with its occupant. It reminded me of Zo's bedroom, with the mix of childhood and teenage decorations, but these were all dusty, abandoned.

"That's the guy who came after me, I think."

I turned around as Elijah spoke. He peered at one of the photos on the wall. He moved back so I could get close enough to look. Three teenagers filled the frame, leaning against each other to pose.

"He was older, but it's him."

"Is that Miss Trager?" The youngest of the three looked like a gangly, thirteen-year-old version of her. My eyes moved to the girl beside her. She didn't look much like Miss Trager here, but I wondered if she was similar enough for me to have mistaken them. Was she the one who had chased me tonight? She had similar pretty features, but they'd landed in a smug, self-assured expression. Adult Miss Trager only ever looked serious and imposing, never smug. In this photo, she just looked awkward and insecure.

My eye moved to the boy in the photo. "So, he must be her brother."

"No shit, Sherlock."

I rolled my eyes, then turned back to the photo. I studied his face, frowning. Even accounting for changes with age, I didn't recognise the boy. "That's not the man I saw."

Which meant *three* people were coming after us, two of them related to Miss Trager. A niggle of doubt scratched at my mind. Were they against her? Perhaps the four of them had been working together to get us back here.

Elijah stared at something else across the room. He pulled another photo from the wall, bringing it over. "Is that Mr Grandace?"

Pulsing thrummed in my ears as he gave it to me. There were six teenagers in the photo this time, three of them Miss Trager and her siblings, then a girl and two other guys – one of them clearly a young, beardless Mr Grandace.

"Yeah, that's definitely him."

Elijah didn't back off this time, instead leaning in to look at the other pictures. The air turned solid between us, making it feel like he was pressing against me. From the way his hand rested in the air above my shoulder, he was doing it on purpose. I focused on the images, ignoring him.

There was something so strange about seeing them like this, standing on the front steps of the school, all of them probably stuck there like we had been. Mr Grandace and Miss Trager were even younger than us, though her siblings looked older. I hadn't been able to picture the teachers as teenagers earlier but seeing it didn't help.

"You reckon this is the original six he told you about?" Elijah asked.

I didn't answer. The man I'd seen outside Zo's house stood next to Mr Grandace in the photo, but that wasn't what gave me pause. The other girl, the one standing in the back behind Miss Trager, was my mother.

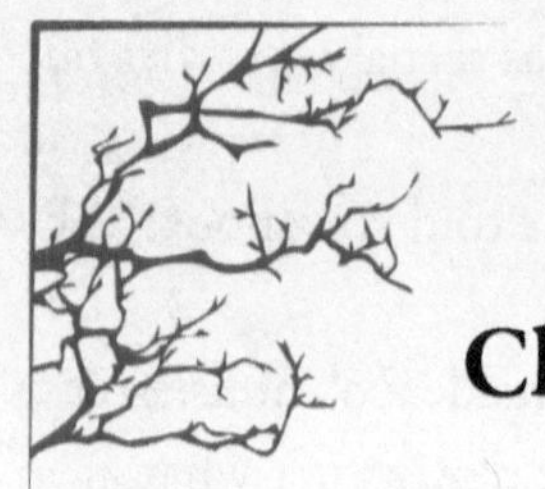

Chapter Eight

"That's my mum." I felt sick. The other implications of that swirled in my head.

"No shit, are you sure?"

"Yes, I'm sure. She looks just like me." Was she even pregnant with me in this photo? Miss Trager mostly hid my mum's stomach, but the way Mum leaned back made me think she could be supporting a rounded belly.

I turned the photo over, reading the names scrawled on the back. *Arthur, Ursula, Chloe, Benjamin, Joseph, and Samantha.* Samantha... Sammy, as my grandmother always called her.

I'd seen photos of her before, of course. Gran had displayed them all over the house. Somehow, seeing her like this was different. I knew she was young when she had me, but it hadn't occurred to me that she was still in school... this school.

Something in my stomach dropped.

Was this why she'd died? Had the school killed her? Mr Grandace said he and Miss Trager were the only survivors – that the others were destroyed by the magic. It was clearly a lie. Miss Trager's siblings were still breathing and so was the man with the dog. Only my mum was gone.

Elijah took the photo from me, holding it up next to my face. "Is Mr Grandace..." A frown creased his brow, and his eyes flicked between me and the image.

"What?" My mouth felt like sandpaper around the word.

"You don't think Mr Grandace is your dad, do you?"

"What? No." I snatched the photo back from him. Mr Grandace's arm draped around my mum. Both of them grinned, her head tipped onto his shoulder. "He can't be... he would have told me, right?"

Elijah shrugged. It was a stupid question. Mr Grandace had lied and kept secrets from the beginning – why would this be any different?

"Could be one of the others," he said. "Miss Trager's brother, maybe. That would make Miss Trager your aunt."

That wasn't any better. Gran hadn't told me much about my father, and it had been long enough that the bits she *had* told me floated just out of reach in my memory. Having so many gaps in my past had always been confusing. Now those gaps felt dangerous, like deep pits that would swallow me if I got too close.

I put the photo down and pressed my hands to my temples. "This is insane."

Elijah stared at me, chewing on his lip. "Don't freak out on me, okay?" He reached out, as if to pat me on the arm, but his hand hovered in the air, not quite touching me.

If our magic hadn't been so determined to force us apart, I would have buried my face in his shoulder and cried, no matter what I thought of him. Right then, I wanted him to hold me – to stroke my hair and say soft soothing things.

I wished Toby were here. He wouldn't get it. He'd grown up in a normal family; no way he'd be able to understand the complexities of what I was feeling. But *he* would have been able to hug me. He would have told me it was going to be all right.

I glanced at Elijah, glad he couldn't read any of that in my thoughts. He'd gone still, staring into the empty air in front of him.

"What's-?"

He yanked me back from the doorway, one arm wrapping around me, the other clapping over my mouth. "Someone's here!" he hissed.

The heat of his skin against mine and the pulsing magic made my head feel like it was going to explode. A scream built inside me, and Elijah tightened his grip reflexively. Somehow the intensity of it helped. I clutched his arm, his muscles tight under my touch, and for a moment the magic seemed to pull me towards him rather than pushing me away.

He let go, inching his hand back, ready to clap it over my lips again if I lost it. I turned towards him, and he held my eye, his gaze intense, but I couldn't tell whether he'd felt the same thing I had.

The floor creaked outside the door, and our heads snapped towards it simultaneously.

"Is it Miss Trager?" I whispered. I never thought I'd see her as the best-case scenario, but her siblings terrified me, and I wasn't quite ready to have the "are you my dad?" conversation with Mr Grandace.

Elijah shook his head. "No, I think it's..." He cut himself off and raced out into the corridor.

I followed. Elijah ran to the right, but the pull took me to the left. I found myself moving towards it automatically, almost as if a hand had wrapped around my wrist, coaxing me along. Static swelled in my head, and I couldn't focus on anything except that pull.

"Cal!" Elijah called.

I shook my head, surprised to find my fingers brushing the glass of the door to the stairs. I turned back. "Sorry, I–" Electricity crackled in the air, and something thudded to the floor in front of Elijah.

"Zo!" he yelled.

I gasped, breaking away from the pull. I quickened my pace, reaching Zo. She shivered, her head rolling to the side. Her skin had paled to a waxy grey, the dark of her spiked hair standing out against it. Elijah tapped her cheek, then her collar bone, but she gave no response.

I crouched down beside her. "Zo... Wake up, Zo." I shook her shoulder. "Can you open your eyes?" She didn't stir, but her chest rose and fell in short breaths.

A second thud sounded, sickeningly loud. I spun around. Julianna lay crumpled at the end of the corridor, her wrist bent at an unnatural angle. Elijah got up, running towards her.

I rolled Zo onto her side, first aid instincts kicking in. "Come on, please wake up." Her arm flopped across her body, lifeless, but the silver of a bracelet glinted at me from her wrist.

The bracelets.

My head shot up. "Elijah, wait!"

He crossed the rune line, and his bracelets snapped together, slamming him into the wall. He fell forward, narrowly missing landing on Julianna's slumped form.

"Elijah!" I ran towards him, screeching to a halt at the rune line. He rolled over onto his back, trying and failing to sit up.

"Are you okay?"

He glared at me. "What do you think?"

"Is Julianna?"

He looked over at her and fell quiet. I couldn't see much from where I stood, but a streak of red slashed across her forehead. A groan sounded from behind me.

"Zo?"

Her breathing turned to gasps, and then to a shriek. I raced back to her. She flailed, not fully conscious yet, only enough to scream. Bruises lined her arms, and a lump formed in my throat. What had I left them to face back at the house?

I put my arm around her, easing her up into a sitting position. Her eyes snapped open, panic filling them. She shoved me off, scrambling back against the wall. Thunder rumbled above us. I moved away, raising my palms, as lightning flashed, and silver sparks rained down on us.

"Hey, hey, Zo. It's me. It's Callie."

She blinked, her eyelids fluttering as her pupils slowly dilated. "Callie. Oh my god, you're here." She crawled towards me, wrapping me in a hug.

"It's okay. It's okay." I rubbed her back. She was trembling, her skin cold to the touch. The storm magistation petered out as she squeezed me tighter, crushing the air out of me. "You were gone."

"I know." Waves of guilt rolled over me again. "I'm sorry. I shouldn't have left."

She let out a sob, and something in my words seemed to register with her. She went still in my arms, then pulled back to look at me. "What do you mean 'left'?" She stared at me, confusion making her eyes wide and childlike.

I couldn't hold her gaze. "I'm sorry. I thought I was doing the right thing."

She shook her head slowly. "We thought they took you. We thought..." She pulled away from me, her voice rising. "You left?! Jules and I were..." Her face paled suddenly. "Where is Jules?"

"Down there. Elijah's with her, but—"

She heaved herself up before I could finish. I lurched after her. "Wait, you can't cross the rune lines." I grabbed her wrist, but she jerked away from me. I grabbed again, locking my arm around her waist.

"Get off me!" She tore at my wrist with her nails, biting into the flesh.

"Woah, listen to her!" Elijah yelled. "I've got Jules, okay?" The bracelets held him in place, but he'd manoeuvred Julianna's head into his lap, his hand clamped against the wound on her forehead.

Zo slowed, her eyes locked on the crimson creeping up between his fingers. "Let me go, she needs me."

Elijah shook his head. "She needs Asher."

Zo flinched, and I tightened my grip. "She needs both of you," I said.

Elijah grimaced. "Yeah, the connection – from both sides."

Zo let out a strangled sound, and her hands flew to her temples. She doubled over, crouching down.

I moved with her, keeping my hand on her back. "Where is he? Was he with you?"

She shook her head, her breath making short, sharp sounds instead of words. She was freezing, and an icy wave of air rushed over me. White flakes of snow danced around her, chilling us both. I never thought I'd miss the sparks of her happy magistations, but we'd all end up with frostbite if she kept this up.

I took her chin in my hand, making her look at me. "What happened?"

She swayed, the blood rushing from her cheeks again. "I don't know... I..." She shivered, her eyes closing. "Sunflowers."

A matching shiver worked its way through me, and not from the cold. "I'm sorry." I could almost see it, the sunflowers growing, lurching their way across the yard and into the house like the vines had; their stalks wrapping around the inhabitants and strangling them.

"Cal..." Elijah met my eye then nodded down at Julianna. A grey tinge marked her skin and the blood from her head dripped down Elijah's wrist.

I put my arms around Zo again, pulling her to her feet. I clasped her face in my hands, forcing her to focus on me. "Where are Toby and Asher?"

She blinked at me, her eyes drifting back to Julianna. I shook her. "Zo! Concentrate! Were they with you? Who sent you here?"

"We... we woke up and you... were gone..." Her voice crack-led, and she took a breath after every second word. Her eyes slid back to mine, finally focusing on me. "Toby and Asher went after you."

I closed my eyes. Of course they had. I'd been stupid to think I could run away without them trying to follow.

"Who sent you here?" I asked Zo. "Was it Miss Trager, or...?"

"Mr Grandace." Zo swallowed, and it was as if her body became solid again. She stopped shaking and words came easier. "There were these people outside. They made the sunflowers grow."

That sounded about right. After their attack on Miss Trager's car failed, they must have gone after the others.

"Do you know if he sent Asher back too?" Elijah asked.

Zo shook her head. "I don't know." She stepped towards Julianna again. "Please let me help her..."

"No." Something forceful swelled in Elijah's voice making her freeze. Her shoulders rocked towards him, as if the momentum of her body would fling her forward with or without her feet following.

"You won't be able to on your own," he said, "and you'll be useless to Julianna if you get stuck like me."

Zo raised her hands in frustration. "We can't just leave her to bleed!"

"Where are Toby and Asher?" I asked again. "You're connected to them – find them."

Elijah blinked as if trying to contact Asher had never occurred to him. Zo swayed on the spot, perhaps too exhausted to even try. I reached out in my own mind, trying to find Toby, but all I found was static.

Elijah let out a breath. "Asher's in the school."

Zo made a sound, but I couldn't tell whether it was laughter or a sob. I wasn't sure which I wanted to do either.

"I can't feel them," she whispered.

I shook my head. "Neither."

"I'm telling you, they're here!" Elijah's voice shot up.

"I believe you," I said. "I just can't..." I barely had the energy to stand, let alone mentally connect with anyone.

"Where?" Zo asked. Her eyes fixed on Julianna, and her voice had lost the crackle, becoming deep and strong.

"Downstairs."

A pang of something painful flashed through me. The pull I'd felt earlier drawing me to that room... what if that's all Elijah was feeling? What if it was still trying to lure us in?

Zo closed her eyes. For a moment, I thought she was going to collapse, then her eyelids snapped open. She turned abruptly, marching down the corridor away from us.

"Zo, wait!" I stumbled into a run.

"Oh yeah, I'm fine," Elijah called after me. "Just leave me here to rot."

I ignored him, and chased after Zo. "Wait, there was something here before. It—"

"I don't care!"

I stepped back, Zo's words hitting me like a physical force. Thunder rumbled around us, bouncing against the walls.

"It's your fault Julianna's hurt. If you'd waited until morning like you'd promised, they wouldn't have gone after you, and we wouldn't have been alone."

I opened my mouth, but it felt like it was full of dust. We stared at each other, and the anger in her eyes didn't burn out. She turned away from me.

"The door's locked," I whispered.

She slammed her hand against it. The glass panel shattered, magic scattering the shards into a perfect circle on the ground. It glinted, catching the light as if it would perform its own set of spells, with or without our help.

Zo reached through the gap, unlocking the door from the other side. She walked through it without looking back. My feet felt heavy, but I pulled them into steps, trailing after her. She thumped down the stairs, but I hesitated on the first one. The pull returned, drawing me down. Maybe it was Toby, calling out to me. He would know what to do. His arms would circle me, the magic weaving us closer together until we were cocooned and safe. He would make everything okay again.

I forced myself down the steps. Below me, Zo walked along an identical corridor to the one we had been on above. She stopped in front of a door, reaching for the handle.

I stumbled as my foot hit the floor, expecting another step. She glanced back but her expression was hard. I righted myself as she turned the handle. A vine crept out from underneath the door.

"Zo!" I bolted down the corridor, but my steps seemed too slow. Vines poured out of the door, smothering her.

"Oh my god, no!" I raced towards her, diving into the tangle of leaves. I grasped her hand, and she clutched mine. "I've got you!" I yelled. "Don't let go!"

But the hand dragged me into the vines with it. "No, stop!" I tried to pull free, but another hand circled my wrist – a male hand, not Zo's.

"Calliope..."

The voice sounded just beside my ear. I whipped around. A face disappeared into the vines – the man from outside Zo's house. His features distorted, gasping for breath. His lips moved, forming words I couldn't make out.

Threads of magic stretched out, pulling me closer, filling my head with static. Vines squeezed my chest, and the air rushed out of me. I went limp, the fight rushing out of me.

He disappeared into the tangle of vines, his hold on me dropping away as we were both swallowed by the plant. He wasn't controlling this. The vines were like Toby's plant, taking over. I had to help him – I had to save both of them.

A spark flashed in front of me, and one of the leaves sizzled, almost catching fire.

"Zo!" I yelled.

More sparks lit up, burning a path through the leaves.

"Hold on Zo. I'm coming." I lunged into the vines. The strands holding me melted, my magic taking over. My hand connected with something, and I felt the brush of Zo's spiky hair, the soft flesh of her cheek. "I'm here! I've got you."

I dived down, finding her shoulder and looping my arm under it. I reached out again, and my fingertips brushed something else. I grabbed it, my hand closing on the man's limp arm.

"Help me, Zo!"

Her magic swelled around mine, and together we pushed backwards, ripping through the vines and out of the room.

Toby! I yelled in my mind. I hoped he could hear me.

I landed on my back, Zo crashing down on top of me, and the man flopped unconscious beside us. Sparks rained down, burning my skin. The vines swarmed above us like a wave. I closed my eyes, not wanting to see when it crashed. Zo turned, clinging to me in a desperate embrace.

"Enough!"

The voice was familiar, but it crackled with power, distorting it. Wind rushed at my face, whipping roughly against my skin. Music came with it, a haunting and disturbing sound.

And then, silence.

I felt the vines retreat, slithering away like cowed children, but I didn't dare look. Footsteps sounded – two sets, maybe more, coming towards us. I creaked my eyes open. A figure crouched down beside me, a grin spreading across his face.

"Can't leave you alone for a second, can I, Reactive Girl?"

"Toby," I whispered.

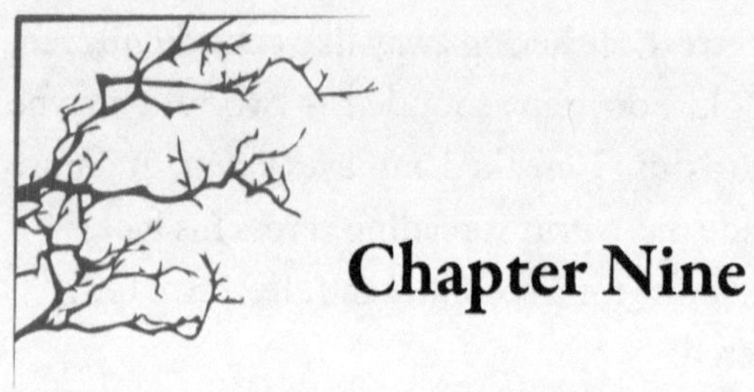

Chapter Nine

Toby guided me back up the stairs, his hand crushing mine as if he thought I would disappear as soon as he loosened his grip. We passed Elijah in the corridor. We'd been freed from the shackles, but he still sat on the floor, leaning back against the wall, his palms pressed to his forehead. I reached out, grabbing his hand as we passed. It made the air around us distort, the pulse bouncing and echoing around us, but he squeezed my hand, clinging to me anyway.

The rest of the school had come alive. Julianna screamed from somewhere down the corridor, and Zo and Asher's voices piled over each other – both trying to comfort her, both doing all they could to heal her wounds.

I stumbled towards the sound. "We have to help her," I said, but Toby held me back.

"There's nothing we can do. Zo and Asher are taking care of her; we'll just be in the way."

I nodded, though it made me feel useless. I hated knowing she was in pain – knowing that it was my fault.

Toby led me into an old living room and planted me on a sofa. A dust sheet covered it, and the end billowed up ghost-like as I sat. The whole room was shielded in similar covers, as if someone hoped it would be forgotten.

A flash of blonde hair raced past the door, followed by the swirl of a black cape. I wanted to run after Miss Trager and Mr Grandace and beg them to explain what was happening, but both teachers looked wild with energy, focused on their own agendas, no time for questions.

I turned back to Toby instead. "I'm sorry," I said.

He just shook his head. "Are you hurt?" he asked.

"I'm fine, are you?"

"Nah, I'm okay."

He wasn't though. A graze ran along the length of his arm. A rip in my jeans revealed a similar one on my knee. I hadn't felt the skin break, but it stung now. Regardless, we were both doing better than Julianna.

"What happened?" My voice came out croaky, my fear of the answer shutting down my voice.

"I don't know about back at the house." He glanced towards the door, Julianna's screams continuing from down the corridor.

"Zo said you and Asher left?"

Zo had told me she and Julianna were alone. What happened to Josh and her parents? Was it too much to hope that the sunflowers had only attacked my friends and left Zo's family unharmed? God, I hoped they were all right.

"We went looking for you and…" Toby swallowed, his face paling just like Zo's had earlier.

I squeezed his hand. "Show me?"

He hesitated, just for a second, but it was long enough for my stomach to drop. Maybe he didn't trust me anymore – I wouldn't blame him if he didn't, after everything that had happened tonight. But then he squeezed my hand back, his mind seeming to open to me, his memories running through it.

It was like watching my own night play out. I saw him running from vines, Miss Trager's brother in the middle of them. How had her siblings been in so many places at once? The obvious answer was magic. Perhaps the people we'd seen attacking us were no more real than the plants.

Would we have been safer if I'd stayed at the house, or would the six of us have become an easier target, taken out in one swoop? We had all been ambushed tonight, that much was obvious, and Miss Trager had saved us. But what exactly had we been saved from? That part seemed to be getting less and less clear as the night went on.

"Mr Grandace pulled me and Asher out of there. Seems like we arrived back just in time." An image of the wave of vines about to crash over me and Zo ran through his head, the memory raw.

I shivered. "The man who made those vines... they swallowed him too," I said. "He made them, but he wasn't in control." His face gasping for air flashed through my mind.

Toby grimaced. "I know. Mr Grandace is dealing with that."

"What...?" The question wouldn't form, exhaustion stealing my words.

Toby moved to kneel in front of me, cupping my face in his hands. I stared at him, focusing only on his eyes.

Are you okay? he said inside his head.

No, I said back.

He nodded, as if that was the only answer he could have expected. *We need to get out of here.*

We can't. I couldn't form the words, not even in my thoughts. Every time I closed my eyes, I saw that wave of vines collapsing over me. I felt the creep of them tightening around me, compressing the air out of my lungs, but more than that I saw the man's face, the way his magic had drawn me in. When he'd spoken to me, I hadn't been able to make out the words, but I was sure he'd been pleading for help.

Why not?

I reached for Toby's hands, clasping them in mine. I tried to transfer it all to him, every memory from the moment I'd left. Toby's eyes widened, and I could see it all playing again in his thoughts.

"My mum," I said aloud. "She was one of them." I needed to know the truth of what happened here. I needed to stop it from happening again.

Toby studied my face. Too many questions raced in his mind. I saw echoes of what had happened to him tonight. His memory of the moment he'd woken and found me gone flashed through his thoughts. I closed my eyes, as if that could stop me feeling everything he had. Instead, his emotions were washed out by my own guilt.

He and Asher had come after me, and they'd gotten caught up in this because of it. Of course, as much as I blamed myself, the real cause was the school. We would never be free of it until we unravelled everything that had happened here.

Finally, Toby nodded. "Then we'll stay." He crawled up onto the couch, wrapping his arms around me.

I laid my head on his chest. The strain on the magical thread between us eased as I listened to his heartbeat. It bounced and fluttered against his ribcage, and I watched flashes of his thoughts. I never should have left him.

Toby lifted his head to look at me. "Why couldn't I hear your thoughts tonight? What was that sound?"

"The static, you mean? You heard it too?"

"Yeah, what was that?" Toby brushed the hair back from my face. "Why couldn't I reach you?"

"I don't know." I dropped my gaze. "Elijah did something – a spell, but I think it was just supposed to make you sleep longer."

"So, it wasn't on purpose?" No judgement filled his voice. His eyes traced over me, no hint of anger in them, but the touch of his fingertips against my temple was hesitant.

"No. I tried reaching for you when everything happened, but you were just gone."

I *had* tried to hide from him, but only with his trick of repeating song lyrics in my head. I had no idea what caused the static. Was it Elijah's magic working against mine? It sounded different to the hum, but perhaps the effect was growing stronger. Or maybe it was the people who had been chasing us – some magical interference, wrapping around me like the vines.

Toby didn't say anything, and eventually I forced myself to look up at him. His Adam's apple bobbed, and I had an urge to run the tip of my finger over it.

"Why did you leave?" His voice was low.

I didn't answer, but I held his eye, letting him read it all in my thoughts. He had to know I hadn't wanted to go. If anything, it had physically hurt to drag myself away. It was more than the magical pull of being bound to him though. He was the person I felt safest with in the whole world and leaving had been like ripping off a limb.

"I shouldn't have," I said aloud.

He swallowed, pulling me back into a hug. His heart rate finally slowed, and I felt mine do the same.

"Stay this time, okay?" he whispered.

I nodded. I wasn't planning on going anywhere.

WE TRIED TO SLEEP, curled up on the couch together. Julianna stopped screaming, but the wailing sound that filled its place was almost worse. Below it, Zo's gentle voice came in shushing waves, soothing all of us. Around us, the school slowly fell quiet, Julianna's tears finally petering out.

I'd never been able to sense anyone except Toby, but my mind kept stretching out, straining to know where each person was. The pull that had drawn me downstairs earlier tickled at the back of my brain, as did a hint of static.

At one point, Elijah made his way down the corridor, and the push of his magic repelling mine pressed against me. He stopped in the doorway, hovering. Somehow it felt too complicated to talk to him. Instead, I pretended to be asleep, and after a few minutes, Elijah walked away. Toby's arms tightened around me as he did.

Eventually, a bar of weak sunlight crept in between the curtains, falling across our faces.

"You awake?" I whispered. I knew he was, but it still felt polite to check.

Toby nodded. "Yeah, couldn't sleep."

"What about the others?"

Toby tilted his head as if listening. "Zo's still with Julianna... actually, I think they all are."

I felt the echoes of all of them in his thoughts. A hint of Julianna's pain filtered through, and he reeled back, distancing himself from Zo's mind to get away from it.

He shifted. "I can still hear it in your head."

"Huh?"

"The static."

The noise had dulled to the point I barely noticed it, but when I listened, it crackled in the background, under the surface of everything.

"It gets louder when you think about those people." Toby rubbed my arm gently, and I focused on the touch.

I hadn't been conscious of thinking about our attackers, but of course they were running through my mind. How could they not be, with everything that had happened?

"Do you think they're causing it? Like the way Elijah and I repel each other?"

"I think Elijah repels everyone." Toby's mouth twisted into a half-smile.

I frowned. A day ago, I would have said the same. But Elijah had saved me several times in the last 24 hours, even with the magic forcing us apart. The memory of him pulling me back from the doorway filled my head. I thought of the heat from his arms wrapping around me, and that moment when the magic had switched. For once it had been drawing me toward Elijah instead of pushing me away... I hadn't imagined it, had I?

Suddenly, Toby flinched. His hand moved to his stomach.

I sat up. "What is it?"

He shook his head. "Nothing – a ping. The magic wants something."

"The magic, or Mr Grandace?"

"Hard to tell. Both I think." He pulled himself into a seated position but didn't get up from the couch.

A trail of fireflies lit up, guiding me out into the corridor – my version of the ping Toby felt when the magic tried to tell him something. We could ignore it. I wasn't sure I was ready to hear anything Mr Grandace had to say, and I certainly didn't trust the magic anymore.

I looked back at Toby. He met my eye, and his hand moved to take mine, clinging to me or comforting me, I wasn't sure.

You jump, I jump, he said inside his head,

He still wanted to run. It didn't matter how much the magic pulled on him, he wanted to fight against it, and honestly, if he'd told me he was leaving, I would have gone with him, no question. But he'd given the decision to me.

"We should follow it." A flood of anxiety rushed through me, but I squashed it down.

He stared at me a moment longer, his breaths slow, almost sighing, then he nodded. "Then we'll follow it."

THE FIREFLIES LED US to a room further down the hallway. Julianna lay scrunched up in a ball on the bed, a faded patchwork quilt spread over her. Asher half-lay beside her, his arms cradling her. Zo sat on the end of the bed. Her hand stretched out, reaching towards Julianna, but she didn't touch her. She looked lost, unsure of her role here. It seemed to hurt her that she couldn't help. She met my eye, briefly, and sparks sizzled around her too quick for me to see the colour.

Miss Trager sat in a corner, her eyes closed. How could she be so calm? How was she unharmed, after everything that had happened last night?

"What is this place?" Toby whispered. "Are we still in the school?"

He stared at the walls. Similar pictures to the ones Elijah and I had found last night lined them, though this time they were peppered with old band posters and pages from magazines. I understood his confusion. The school nestled in the remnants of an old home – Miss Trager's childhood home. No wonder they had kept us so confined when we were students – or should I say prisoners – here. So many questions needed answers, but I doubted we would get satisfactory ones.

Toby and I both jumped at a creaking door, out in the corridor. Footsteps sounded, and Toby stepped in front of me, his hands raised. A pulse started behind my eyes.

"It's just Elijah," I said.

Toby didn't relax his stance, but he lowered his hands.

The hum intensified, as Elijah came through the doorway. He smirked, almost letting it turn into a genuine smile when he met my eye. Then his gaze flicked to Toby, and his eyes narrowed. He took a step towards Asher instead, but then stopped himself. Asher didn't look up, his attention fully absorbed in Julianna. Elijah hovered for a moment, and then he sat down on the end of the bed next to Zo.

She gave him a half-smile and looked back at Julianna and Asher. Elijah and I might be the ones on the ends, but the two of them were the ones being shoved aside.

"I'm glad you're okay," I told him.

His lips flicked back into a smirk. "Course I'm okay. I always am."

That was probably true. Silence fell over us again. A sense of expectation filled the room. It couldn't be a coincidence Elijah had turned up here now. He must have been called by the magic too. Each breath we took seemed to hang, all of us waiting.

Mr Grandace strode into the room, breaking the tension. There were no warning door creaks or footsteps this time; perhaps his magic gave him the advantage of a silent approach. He didn't spare us even the briefest of glances, going straight to Miss Trager. He reached out, stopping short of touching her. She looked up, and her lips parted, but she didn't speak. They were both frozen, locked in eye contact and in each other.

I wondered if they could talk to each other inside their heads in the same way Toby and I did. It seemed like they were playing out a similar conversation to the one Toby and I had just had.

Mr Grandace finally drew his eyes away from her, and scanned the room, looking at each of us in turn. His eyes fell on me and lingered there. I couldn't read his expression. Regret? Relief? Guilt? Honestly, I didn't care what he was feeling. All I could think of was that picture of his arm wrapped around my mother.

I found my mouth opening. "You lied to me." I didn't plan to say it, the words burst out of me.

Mr Grandace blinked, confusion washing all of the other conflicting expressions away. "I promise you I haven't, Calliope."

"You told me the rest of your circle were dead. You said you and Miss Trager were the only survivors."

Miss Trager flinched. She didn't make a sound, but she bit her lip so hard it turned white. Mr Grandace touched her arm, gently, and the rest of what I wanted to say died on my tongue.

She didn't have any makeup on, and her hair fell in messy, frizzy coils over her face. I'd never seen her like that. For once, she seemed almost human. She swallowed, about to cry, which scared me more than anything else.

"I never said they died," Mr Grandace said, quietly. "We're the only ones who survived unscathed."

Toby caught my eye. He shook his head, his jaw clenched tightly. *Unscathed.* That was a fancy way of skirting around the obvious damage that had been caused to the others. Why couldn't he tell us the truth? What could be so bad that he had to dance around it like this?

"One of our circle died," Miss Trager said, almost as if she were reminding him. "The rest were... lost to the magic."

Elijah scoffed. "So that's why your crazy brother and sister are running around trying to kill us?"

Asher looked up, finally drawing his gaze away from Julianna. Zo shifted and murmured something under her breath. Of course – the others didn't know about the photos Elijah and I had found.

"They're not crazy," Miss Trager said quietly.

I could almost have felt sorry for her. But she was still lying to me. They were both still lying.

"By one of your circle, you mean my mother." The words tasted like chalk in my mouth.

Mr Grandace's eyes flicked up to meet mine, and Miss Trager took in a sharp breath. I stared back at them, willing them to try and lie again.

"Your mother..." Zo trailed off, and the rest of my classmates shifted, their eyes locked on me.

Toby's hand slipped into mine. I squeezed it tight. Questions circled me, filtering through Toby's thoughts. I ignored them, focusing only on my former teachers.

Mr Grandace cleared his throat. "There's a lot you don't understand, Callie." His voice was low... haunted. He looked to Miss Trager, and she shook her head.

"She was a part of our circle," she said. "She was my friend." Her voice cracked on that final word.

I swallowed. Elijah's question from earlier burned in my throat – was he my father? Was she my aunt? The words stuck in my chest, refusing to come out. I couldn't hold Mr Grandace's eye any longer.

"Samantha – your mother – was important to us, Calliope. She was our friend, and her magic was incredibly powerful. We didn't even know *how* powerful at the time." Mr Grandace hesitated again. He moved forward, his steps jerky and unnatural. "She... she wrote the prophecy."

I reeled back. Toby's grip tightened on my hand, the only thing anchoring me.

"Callie's mother wrote..." Zo trailed off. The others were all talking at once, and the noise seemed to slam against me.

My mother wrote the prophecy. She was the reason Mr Grandace brought me to the school, and the reason Miss Trager had tried to kill Toby.

Suddenly, one more thing became clear. My mother had died because of this – because of the magic. Quite possibly, one of the other people in her circle had killed her. And if we weren't careful, the same thing would happen to us.

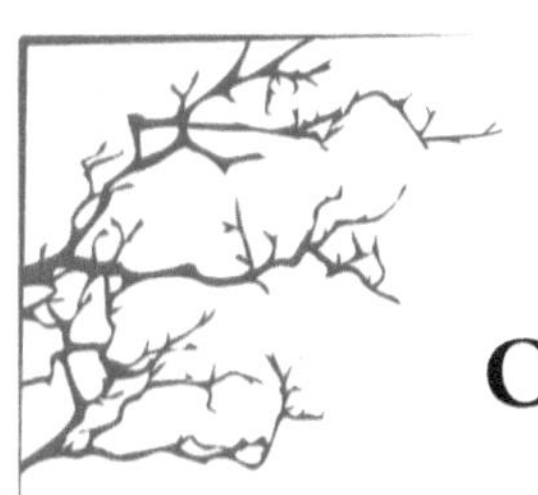

Chapter Ten

The others asked questions, but it was too much – too many aspects that needed to be explained. Mr Grandace's jaw clenched, and he kept shaking his head before answering. I wanted to know about my mother, of course I did. But a much more pressing question circled in my mind.

"What is it you want us to do?"

Somehow, my voice broke through the noise. The others fell quiet and Mr Grandace's face relaxed, almost but not quite smiling. I met Toby's eye. The idea of running consumed his thoughts again. I drew my gaze away, not letting myself consider it.

"I want to link the two circles together," Mr Grandace said.

The feeling of the strands of magic wrapping around me engulfed me. My connection with Toby pulled tight, and the frayed ends of my broken tie to Elijah tingled as if they would regrow.

"No way." Toby's voice was firm, cold almost. He slipped his arm around my waist, but it did nothing to ease the tension on the threads of magic.

"But we're already linked," Zo said. I could almost see her connections to Toby and Julianna lighting up.

Mr Grandace nodded. "I know, but the prophecy suggests—"

"The prophecy suggested killing Toby." Asher pulled Julianna closer, wrapping his arm around her. We were all moving in again, closing ranks against our former headmaster. "It's clearly all bull."

My mother wrote the prophecy... It wasn't possible.

"The prophecy never told me to kill Toby." Miss Trager didn't look up. "I was trying to stop what she'd predicted from happening."

Suddenly, she seemed so small, no different to the teenager in the photo. She'd always been so imposing, terrifying even. Now she just seemed afraid.

"The magic is unbalanced," Mr Grandace continued. "Both circles are missing links – between you and Elijah," he gestured to me, "and where your mother would have been in our circle. The prophecy talks about intersecting circles – *none will be complete until all interlink.*"

He said that last part as if quoting. I looked to Elijah, but he didn't return my gaze. He stared at Mr Grandace.

"If we'd known to link ourselves back then," Mr Grandace said, "maybe we could have controlled the magic better, but..."

But my mother's prophecy hadn't told them to. Or maybe it had, and they hadn't listened.

"If we join both circles together, we think it will stabilise all of us. But we need you to be in agreement. The others in our circle..." Mr Grandace hesitated, and Miss Trager grimaced. "The power has corrupted them. They won't be willing to give it up easily," he said finally.

If tonight was anything to go by, that was an understatement. They were clearly willing to fight or even kill us to keep the status quo.

They killed my mother...

How had it happened? Was it an accident or had they meant to hurt her? I thought of the photo of the six of them, all so young and fragile. One day, would I look back at a photo of the six of us and think the same? Would I even get the chance?

"I know you all have so many questions," Mr Grandace said as if he had heard my thoughts. "I promise you, I will answer all that I can, but joining the circles is urgent. Ursula and I can't keep the others contained for much longer."

The wave of vines flashed through my head again, and the face of the man swallowed by them. By keeping them contained, he didn't just mean locking them up. The magic was overwhelming them, and they were all drowning in it.

Mr Grandace cleared his throat. "We'll leave you alone to decide." His eyes were on me, but I didn't look up.

He put his arm around Miss Trager, guiding her out of the room. She leaned on him heavily, limping. So much for my belief that she was unharmed, though the biggest damage was to our view of her. All I could see now was that tiny teenage girl from the photo.

Toby stood as soon as they were gone. "There's no way we're doing this."

"Why not?" Elijah's voice was level but filled with a bitterness. "At least we're getting a choice this time."

I blinked at Elijah's words. I hadn't expected him to be on the teachers' side. But perhaps he wasn't on *their* side, just against Toby's.

Toby shook his head. "I had to link us; you know that. We all would have died if I hadn't."

"So you say." Elijah's gaze fixed on Toby, but I felt him pull at the frayed edges of our severed connection, almost as if he were trying to speak to me through it. Funny how I could still feel it, even after it broke. Would the connection between us regrow, or would I be joined to Mr Grandace or one of the others? Nausea flooded me at the thought.

"I think I want to do it." Julianna raised her head, too weak to sit up properly. It was the first time she'd spoken, and we all turned to stare at her. "I want this to be over."

Zo and Asher didn't say anything, but it was like I could see the connections light up again. They both loved Julianna enough to follow her, no matter what they actually wanted to do.

"We can't trust them!" Toby's voice strained. His eyes flicked to mine, pleading. "He said we have to all be in agreement."

Zo scoffed. "Like that's ever going to happen."

"Well, it's going to have to." Asher's raised voice silenced everyone.

"What do you want to do, Cal?" Elijah's voice was steady, none of his usual snark. All eyes turned to me, both Elijah and Toby expecting me to side with them. Whichever way I went, Toby would follow me, same as Asher and Zo followed Julianna. I could turn this into a consensus, or I could hold out and maybe save us.

I swayed on the spot, exhaustion catching up with me. Toby stepped towards me, but I held out my hand, stopping him. "I want to read the prophecy."

I HEADED DOWN THE CORRIDOR to the bathroom while Toby went to find Miss Trager. I didn't really need to go; it was an excuse to take a breath. Everything Mr Grandace had told us was just... it was a lot of information to get in a short space of time.

The picture of my mother with Miss Trager and Mr Grandace haunted me. They had been friends. I'd had no idea my mother had magic, though that wasn't surprising. I'd had no idea *I* had magic before a few months ago.

I needed time, but I wasn't going to get it. What if I made the wrong choice? I felt like I'd been spinning for so long making wrong decision after wrong decision. Toby binding us together had made things better – it had saved us at the school, but it hadn't been the right thing for us since then. I didn't know if binding us to more people would be either.

I splashed some water on my face and stared at myself in the mirror. Julianna was right. This needed to be over.

I opened the door to the corridor. Miss Trager stood right outside, and I stumbled back a pace. She'd tidied herself up a bit, smoothing back the frizzy hair at least, but the paleness of her skin betrayed how worn out she was.

"Toby said you wanted to see the prophecy," she said.

I nodded. Toby hovered further down the corridor, Elijah behind him. Toby would see the pages in my mind, and he could pass them on to the others, but they were giving me the space to do this on my own. I wasn't sure what I was looking for, but somehow, I felt it would help if I could see it in her words.

Miss Trager gave a mouth shrug, then put her hand on my shoulder, gently guiding me back towards the room where we'd found the photos. I'd never seen her as anything remotely maternal, but knowing she knew my mother – that she could be my aunt – the touch felt more affectionate. I shrugged away, not willing to feel that from her.

I hovered in the doorway while she sat down on the bed, opening a drawer in the base of it. She ruffled through the contents, pulling out an old makeup palette and a couple of grubby soft toys. She placed them gently on the bed beside her, as if they still meant something to her.

I looked away, picking up the photo of the six of them again and studying my mother's face. This was Miss Trager's room – her childhood room, which meant she lived here even before it became a school. There was something so strange about seeing evidence of her being human, especially seeing them all together in the picture. I glanced over at her. She'd shrunk before my eyes. I couldn't see her as an adult anymore – just a fragile teenage girl, as helpless as me.

She pulled out a stack of battered exercise books and flicked through them. "Here." She selected one of the books from the pile, but she didn't hand it to me, clutching it in both her hands on her lap instead.

I hesitated, then walked over, sitting down on the bed beside her.

She took a heavy breath, trying not to cry. "You're so like her, Callie. I..."

She didn't finish that, but I was sure she'd been going to say she missed her. I didn't know what to say in response. I couldn't tell her that I understood. I'd never known my mum. I missed the *idea* of her, but that was all I had.

"I'm not trying to keep things from you, but you may not be able to read it."

"Why not?"

Miss Trager's fingers tightened on the edges of the book, biting into them. "The way your mother wrote... she said you could only read her words when you needed them the most."

That sounded like some new-age hippie bunk. Was that what my mother was like? Swanning around writing enigmatic prophecies no one could read?

Miss Trager placed the book on my lap. "Here," she said again. "I don't know if you'll find what you're looking for, but there it is."

She stood quickly and moved out of the room, her hands flying to her face as if she was ashamed to let her tears fall.

Doodles and scribbled words crisscrossed the cover of the book. I made out the names of her classmates, and that strange "S" everyone draws. But mostly she'd drawn circles. Layers and layers of them, overlapping. Apart from that, it looked like a normal exercise book, like one of mine from my old school. So strange that a prophecy that had nearly gotten us killed would be written in something so ordinary.

I flipped the book open, trying to read a page at random. The writing scrawled over the page in a stream-of-conscious-ness rant. Again, this wasn't what I'd expected. Strings of letters dripped and weaved over the lines, some of them barely legible.

Certain words and phrases had been underlined, and notes made in the margins.

I understood what Miss Trager meant about not being able to read it. Though I could see it was written in English, the words seemed to move, impossible to focus on. A few lines jumped out at me.

Siren plant...

...all six survive or none of them do...

...catastrophic power...

I ran my hand over the page. There was something so perverse about this. Our whole lives had been upended because of this – the handwritten ramblings of a girl not much older than me.

The girl will know only that her mother died, and her grandmother raised her.

The next line blurred, disappearing just as I tried to read it.

She will live sixteen summers, and on her seventeenth birthday, the sky will burst into fire, and it will begin.

Why was the book only showing me things that had already happened? They weren't exactly prophecies anymore. Perhaps it would have been nice to know I was going to set Zo's ceiling on fire before things got out of control, though I'm not sure I could have stopped it.

...only the sacrifice can save them...

...She will be tuned to the family, and she will choose them...

The family? She was my only family, and she was gone. I flicked through the pages, but nothing else became clear, the words remaining disjointed scrawls. I couldn't find the bit about circles Mr Grandace had quoted, though I kept scanning the pages for it.

Maybe this was a lost cause. I'm not sure seeing it would make the words more meaningful anyway. I had to make this decision for myself – I wasn't going to get any guidance from these pages, and definitely not from my long-dead mother.

My eye fell on the annotations in the margins. They'd been written by someone else in a different colour pen. It wasn't the words themselves that caught my attention; it was the handwriting. The same handwriting from the birthday cards I'd gotten every year from my father.

"What do you mean, you let her look at it?"

I looked up at the sound of Mr Grandace's voice in the corridor. Miss Trager said something in response, but I couldn't hear it over the thumping of my own pulse. Or maybe that was his footsteps, pounding down the corridor towards me.

I stood, clutching the book to my chest.

I thought of trying to run again, but I couldn't do that to Toby or to Zo, or to any of them. Even Elijah had grown on me and become part of the weird family we'd created.

I forced my feet into steps. Mr Grandace appeared in the doorway, meeting me halfway.

"Calliope." He strode towards me, his arms reaching out as if to pull me into a hug, or maybe to rip the book from my hands.

"She wanted to see for herself." Miss Trager stopped outside the room. She looked from Mr Grandace to me. Shivers worked their way up my body, and I clung tighter to the book – to my mother.

"I'm sorry. She shouldn't have let you try and read that. It's too much." He placed a hand on my arm, his touch gentle, like Miss Trager's had been. It made me shiver more.

I stared at him, trying to find something familiar in his face. "Are you...?" I couldn't get the words out.

His eyes dropped to the notebook. He reached for it, but I held it back.

"The cards," I said. "Are you...?" But I still couldn't say it.

He reached for the prophecy again, but I didn't let him touch me. I could feel the fizzing of energy coming from his skin. It may have been meant to be soothing, to manipulate me into being calm, like the clouds of coloured energy Toby said he used to send out at the school. All it did was make me angry.

"My father sent me birthday cards," I forced out. "The handwriting..."

Understanding finally dawned on his face. Miss Trager made a noise in her throat. She came closer and I let her. I wasn't sure when she had become the more trustworthy of the two, but I found myself moving towards her, wanting the comfort of someone who had loved my mother.

"I'm not your father, Calliope," he said.

I wasn't sure whether to believe him. He and Miss Trager had lied and omitted and stretched the truth so many times. He reached for the notebook again, and this time I let him take it, along with the photo.

His expression fell, and he ran his thumb over the faces of the six of them. He opened the book, tracing the lines of writing as if he understood far more of it than I ever could.

He looked up at me. "But I did write those cards. I'm sorry."

I shook my head. "Why?"

Miss Trager cleared her throat. She moved closer to me again, and I let her. She pointed to the third boy in the photo.

"Joseph... he's your father. He was a part of the original circle. He and your mother came to the school together."

Not Miss Trager's brother, but the man with the dog. The one who had been watching me and started those sunflowers growing, triggering all of this. The one who had nearly drowned us both in the wave of vines.

"He's one of the bad ones," I said. The words choked me.

"No... no." Mr Grandace took hold of my shoulders. "Your father is not a bad person," he said firmly. "None of them are. The magic, it..."

It had taken him over, just as it would take all of us over if we let it. I thought of the way he'd reached for me – saying my name as if asking for help. Maybe he had been asking for help all along.

"Ursula and I, we promised your mother we would look after you. She loved you very much."

Miss Trager nodded, her eyes filling with tears, and I found I believed them.

"Your father... he knew the magic was going to take him over. He wanted us to make sure you knew he was alive – that he still loved you. We didn't know how else..." Mr Grandace's voice petered out, perhaps realising it was a pathetic explanation. "We couldn't do much else. We didn't want him to find you."

I heard the unspoken end of that. My father had loved me and wanted me to know that once upon a time, but now the magic had taken him over he was just a danger to me. The one good memory I had of him was those birthday cards, and he hadn't even written them.

"This is why we need to link the two circles," Miss Trager said. "We can bring them back to us – my brother and sister, and your father. We can fix what the magic broke, like Samantha wanted."

Mr Grandace raised the notebook in his hand, as if to invoke her. He made it sound so simple, but was it? Did he really believe he could bring my father back after all these years?

Toby appeared in the doorway. He looked between me and the teachers. *Are you okay?* he asked me inside his head.

I didn't answer, because honestly, I didn't know. "Can I talk to him?" I asked.

Miss Trager winced. She opened her mouth to answer, but Mr Grandace spoke over her. "It's not a good idea. You saw what happened last time."

Toby's memory of finding me covered in vines flashed through his head. I understood why he was afraid, but surely there were ways we could make it safe? If Zo hadn't opened that door, we wouldn't have been overwhelmed.

I wondered if she had forgiven me, now Julianna was healed. Somehow, I didn't think it was really about that. I'd been beginning to think of her as family, but she'd kept her feelings for Julianna a secret from me, and then practically cast me out when Julianna got hurt. Perhaps we had never been that close after all.

"He's asleep right now. We used a spell on all of them," Miss Trager added. She stared at me, and I got the feeling there was something else she wanted to say. Would she have answered differently, had Mr Grandace given her the chance?

"It's time," Mr Grandace told me. "We need to link the two circles."

He didn't ask if I'd made my decision – didn't ask if any of us had. Somehow, he seemed to know it had all come down to me, and he was sure he had me onside.

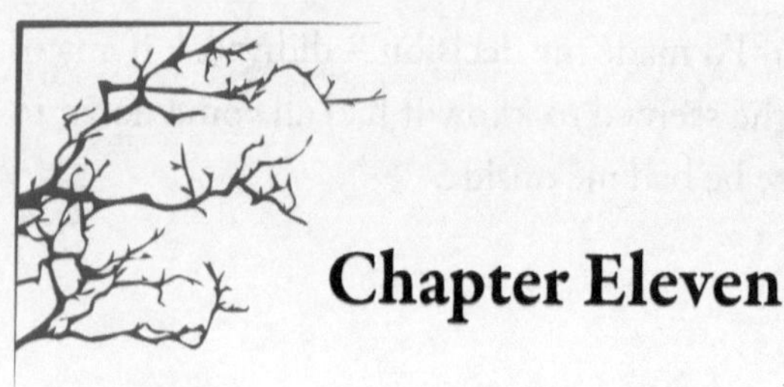

Chapter Eleven

My classmates made slow, limping progress down the corridor. Julianna could barely stand. Dried blood coated her clothes in blotches, like a brown floral pattern, and flecks of red speckled her face. She clung to Asher and Zo, and they bore her weight on each step.

The glass from where Zo had broken the door had scattered across the floor, her perfect circle destroyed by running feet. Toby and I swept it into a pile in the corner, then stood in front of it, like we were protecting a glittering hoard. In reality, we just hoped to save our classmates' bare feet from being shredded.

Downstairs, my father was a prisoner, just like I had been at the school. Magic had been forced on me. Was I really about to do the same to him? I didn't know if this was the right thing. Would he be free once we joined the circles? How could he be after he and Miss Trager's siblings had been responsible for my mother's death?

Mr Grandace and Miss Trager crouched on the floor of the corridor below, laying rune lines. Supposedly they would keep us safe as we bound the circles. The teachers had asked us to give them twenty minutes to lay the magic, and then to follow them down there. It had taken nearly that long to get Julianna this far.

She reached the broken door and let out a little high-pitched groan at the sight of the stairs. Her legs gave way, and she slumped against Asher.

"Jules!" Zo dived forward to grab her, but Asher scooped Julianna up, pushing Zo away as he did.

"I've got her."

Julianna made another noise, as if in pain, but her head fell against Asher's shoulder, relieved at not having to walk any further.

"It's okay," Asher told her. "This will be over soon." He glanced at me and Toby, and the look in his eyes was a challenge.

He carried Julianna down the stairs, disappearing into darkness at the bottom.

Zo hesitated. Her arms dangled at her sides, as if she wasn't sure what to do with them, now she wasn't supporting Julianna.

"Zo, I–"

She half turned towards me then cut the movement short. Her head froze at an odd angle, as if she was trying to pretend she hadn't heard me. She kept it there as she drifted down the stairs, more willing to risk tripping than accidentally making eye contact with me.

Toby squeezed my arm. "She'll be okay. She just needs time."

He was wrong. Zo was cutting me out, the same way so many families had done before. Even if he had been right, time wasn't something I could give when we were all linked to each other. In a few minutes, we would be linked to even more people – to my father. Would I feel more of a familial connection to him once the magic joined us? The idea of being able to read his thoughts terrified me.

Toby pulled me into a hug. I leaned into him, resting my head on his chest. In all honesty, I was scared of losing this. Even though it was hard sometimes, being linked just to Toby felt special. I had lost so much already. Would we still have this closeness if I was attached to someone else on the other side?

He pulled back to look at me. *You could never lose me, Reactive Girl.* He brushed the hair back from my face, his touch gentle.

I kissed him. I felt his surprise, then he was kissing me back. The feel of his lips mixed with the sensation of mine meeting his, each of us experiencing it from both sides. I pulled him closer, until I couldn't separate where my skin ended and his began.

The sound of a throat clearing startled me. I sprung back, spinning around. Elijah stared at us from the stairs, an expression I couldn't read crossing his face.

"If you're quite done, they're almost ready," he said.

I nodded, my face flushing. Neither Toby nor I made any move to go downstairs, though.

Elijah hesitated. His gaze flicked between me and Toby, finally landing on me. Heat rose in my cheeks, and I found I couldn't hold his eye. The severed end of the thread between us tingled, as if trying to regrow. Toby's arm slid around my waist, the pressure of his touch comforting.

Elijah cleared his throat again. "We need to do this, Cal. It's the only way."

I hadn't realised my hesitation was so obvious. Elijah turned, making his way back down the stairs.

Toby turned to me, stepping in close again. I rested my forehead against his. *Are you sure?* he said in his mind.

I shook my head. *No, but what other choice do we have?*

Since when did I trust Elijah over Toby? My gut told me we shouldn't be doing this, but my father... this might be my only chance to bring him back.

Toby dropped his gaze. He didn't try to hide his reservations, and I read it all in his thoughts. Finally, he looked up at me. "I trust you."

I could tell it was true. He didn't want to do this – didn't believe for a second that our former teachers had our best interests at heart – but he trusted me enough to follow me. He pressed his lips lightly against mine again. *You jump, I jump, right?*

I found his hand, and we walked down the stairs together.

MISS TRAGER CROUCHED in front of the door where my father was being held, adjusting the chalk rune lines. Identical lines ran in front of the doors on either side, presumably trapping her siblings inside.

She stood as we came downstairs, giving me a half-smile. "Good timing."

I nodded. My voice didn't seem to be working.

"Here." Mr Grandace took Julianna's arm and helped her to lean against the wall, opposite the door. He arranged the others on either side of her into a semi-circle. He gestured for me and Toby to take our places. Zo, Julianna, and Asher linked up, holding hands following the lines of magic.

I looked over at Elijah. He stood between Asher and Miss Trager with both hands in his pockets. I met his eye, and he nodded once. He took hold of Miss Trager and Asher's hands, completing his arc of the circle.

I turned to Toby. "It'll be okay. We'll be okay." My voice was not convincing, a tremor running through it.

His shoulders slumped, deflating, but he linked up with Zo anyway. I'd known he would follow me, whichever way I chose. It didn't make me feel any better about it, though.

"Thank you, all of you," Mr Grandace said.

I thought I sensed a little of that calming magic Toby had talked about floating out from him. "We're not doing it for you." I held out my hand, but he didn't take it.

"You won't be linked to me," he said. "You'll be linked to your father."

My stomach lurched. I thought of his hand, pulling me into the wave of vines, and I could almost feel them regrowing, slithering over my body.

"We're going to have to wake them," Miss Trager said. "So once we start, do not let go under any circumstances. We'll need to work the magic as quickly as possible."

A flash of fear passed around the room. Mr Grandace and Miss Trager looked at each other. Years of stress, tiredness, and connection seemed to pass through their eyes. Then there was a click as the spell dropped away.

Even though I wasn't connected to him yet, I felt my father wake. I could hear all three of them moving around on the other side of those doors. I gripped Toby's hand so tightly, it hurt us both, but I didn't want him to let go. He squeezed back just as intensely. Fear rolled inside him, anxious thoughts bouncing through all of us.

Mr Grandace's magic sent out a call. Julianna and Zo's magic resisted at first, then it intertwined with his. He moved on to Asher and Toby. Elijah and I would be next. I took a breath, trying to let my mind relax, to let my magic flow ready to answer Mr Grandace's call.

It wasn't the same as when Toby had done it. Then, it had almost been automatic, the reactive magic taking over. This felt forced, unnatural. But Elijah was right – what other choice did we have? We couldn't spend our lives running from Miss Trager's siblings and my father, nor could we leave their magic to continue destroying them and anyone else they came into contact with.

Perhaps this would be good. Perhaps the two of us would finally feel connected, instead of the horrible push we always had against each other. I tried to imagine how it would be. Each of us balanced, no longer being dragged towards Toby and repelled away from Elijah.

I squeezed Toby's hand, and he opened his eyes, meeting mine. Mr Grandace's magic reached out for me, and Toby gave me a nod. This would be okay. It had to be.

Something invisible slammed into me. I opened my mouth to scream, but nothing came out, my body winded by the force. A second slam threw me backwards, and my hand ripped out of Toby's. Elijah flew backwards too, the magical force repelling him as well.

Static shrieked around me. I clutched my ears, trying to block it out.

Toby ran towards me. "Callie!" his lips said, but there was no sound.

I reached for him, and he was flung backwards, hit by the wall of magic. I felt the wave of it slamming into me again.

Toby! I screamed.

Calliope, I heard in amongst the noise, but it wasn't Toby.

I tried to scramble up, but the static exploded in my head, even louder than before, bringing me to my knees. I reached for the thread tying me to Toby. It flung me back again. I stared at the others; all of them sprawled on the floor, their faces peering at me in identical shock.

For once, I could see all of the magic around us. Tattered strings of it hung in the air. New threads reached out. They wrapped around me, drawing me in. I felt a familiar pull, but it wasn't bringing me closer to Toby.

Come here, Calliope, fuzzy words formed in the static, voices becoming clearer, like a radio tuning in on a station. I felt my magic responding to it. I tried to fight, but I couldn't move. My magic reached out, independent of me. The threads bound me, wrapping tighter and tighter until I couldn't move or speak.

And then, suddenly, the static was gone.

Hello, my daughter. The voice was clear. I felt myself turning, my head moving without my permission.

"The circle is complete," Elijah said, but it didn't sound like his voice. He turned, walking to the locked door and opening it. His movements were jerky, robotic. He unlocked the next door, then the third.

No one else moved. Everything seemed to be in slow motion, all of us suspended in a strange, liminal space. Miss

Trager's sister walked out of one of the rooms. She stared at me, with the smug, self-satisfied grin I'd seen in the photo of her.

And then my father appeared. I found myself standing, greeting him with a hug. I fought against it, but I wasn't in control of my own limbs.

"Callie!" Toby stared up at me, from where he'd fallen.

No resonance filled his words, the sound dull and hollow. A sickening realisation grew inside me. I heard only his external voice. I couldn't hear his thoughts anymore. I tried to reach for him, but I couldn't move.

Heaviness filled my mind. Toby's image blurred in front of me. Some part of my brain told me I should be worried about him, that I was still tied to him and wanted to be near him, but more than that I wanted to be near these people – near my father. Their magic wrapped around me like a hug.

"I have to go," I heard myself saying.

Elijah took one of my hands, and my father took the other. "Callie!"

I heard Toby's voice, but there was no Callie now. We walked away, leaving the old circle behind us.

End of Book Two

Enjoyed this book? You can make a big difference.

REVIEWS ARE THE MOST powerful tool when it comes to getting attention for my books.

As an indie author, it can be hard to get my books into the hands of readers, but honest reviews help me do just that.

If you've enjoyed this book, I would be very grateful if you could spend just a few minutes leaving a review (it can be as short as you like).

Thank you very much!

Review on Goodreads

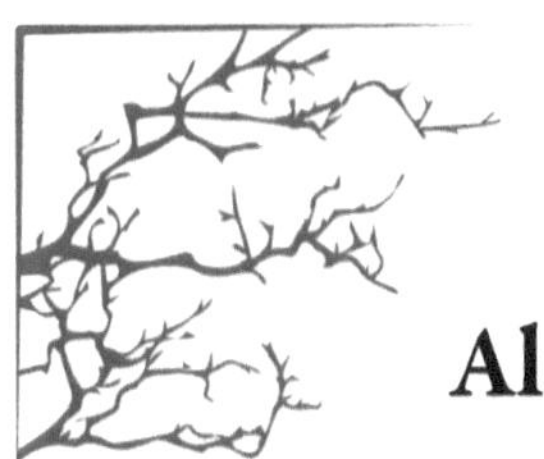

Also by Helen

Reactive Magic Series

Reactive

Magnetic

Familiar Magic Series

Familiars and Foes

Accidents and Apparitions (published in Jingle Spells)

Curses and Cousins

Young Adult Books

Broken Silence

Underwater

We All Fall

Children's Books

The Trespassers Club

There's No Such Thing As Humans

Aunt Kelly's Dog

Jenny No-Knickers

Do Fruit Worry About Getting Fat?

Short Stories

Symbolic Death

Find out more at www.helenvfletcher.com

Coming soon...
Volatile: Reactive Magic Book 3
Seventeen years ago, it all began...
Join Helen's mailing list at www.helenvfletcher.com to be one
of the first to read it.

About the Author

Helen Vivienne Fletcher is a children's and young adult author, spoken word poet and award-winning playwright. She has won and been shortlisted for numerous writing competitions including winning the Outstanding New Playwright Award at the Wellington Theatre Awards, making the shortlist for the Storylines Joy Cowley Award, and the finalist list for the Ngaio Marsh Best First Book Award.

Helen has worked in many jobs, doing everything from theatre stage management to phone counselling. She discovered her passion for writing for young people while working as a youth support worker, and now helps children find their own passion for storytelling through her work as a creative writing tutor.

She lives in Wellington with her disability assistance dog, Bindi – a five-year-old, playful Labrador who loves soft toys, cuddles, and can fit three tennis balls in her mouth at once.

Overall, Helen just loves telling stories and is always excited when people want to read or hear them.

Read more at https://www.helenvfletcher.com/.